**Fredonia Books
Amsterdam, The Netherlands**

The Heart of the Serpent:
Soviet Science Fiction

by
Ivan Yefremov
Arkady Strugatsky
Boris Strugatsky
et al.

ISBN: 1-4101-0041-3

Copyright © 2002 by Fredonia Books

Fredonia Books
Amsterdam, The Netherlands
http://www.fredoniabooks.com

All rights reserved, including the right to reproduce this book, or portions thereof, in any form.

In order to make original editions of historical works available to scholars at an economical price, this facsimile of the original edition is reproduced from the best available copy and has been digitally enhanced to improve legibility, but the text remains unaltered to retain historical authenticity.

CONTENTS

Ivan Yefremov. The Heart of the Serpent . . . 5

Anatoly Dnieprov. Siema 115

Victor Saparin. The Trial of Tantalus 165

Valentina Zhuravleva. Stone from the Stars . . 207

Arkady and Boris Strugatsky. Six Matches . . 232

IVAN YEFREMOV

THE HEART OF THE SERPENT

Music broke through the mists of oblivion. "Awake, ye, yield not to sinister entropy...." The words of the familiar song stirred memories and started off an endless chain of accustomed associations.

Life returned to the great ship. It still trembled, but the automatic devices went on with their work. The whirls of energy that had enveloped the three beehive-shaped green metal domes in the control room had died down. In a few seconds the domes leapt up and disappeared in niches overhead among a maze of pipes, trusses and wires, revealing three men reclining in deep padded seats.

Two of the men remained motionless, but the third stirred, opened his heavy-lidded eyes and tossed back a mane of dark hair. He raised himself up from the depths of the soft insulation, and leaned forward to read the multitude of dials on the slanting illuminated surface of the main instrument panel that stretched across the compartment half a metre in front of the three seats.

"So we're out of the warp," he heard a strong voice say next to him. "I see you are again the first to awake, Kari. You really have the ideal constitution for an astronaut!"

Kari Ram, electronics engineer and astronavigator of the space ship *Tellur*, turned sharply to meet the still clouded gaze of the ship's captain, Moot Ang.

The captain shifted his position with an effort,

sighed with relief and turned his attention to the panel.

"Twenty-four parsecs*.... We've passed right by a star. New instruments are always inaccurate ... or perhaps I should say we haven't learned to use them properly yet. You can cut off the music —Tey's awake."

In the silence that fell Kari Ram could distinctly hear the uneven breathing of the man who had just regained consciousness.

The main control room was a good-sized circular chamber safely hidden deep in the bowels of the space ship. Above the instrument panels and hermetically sealed doors a bluish screen ran all round the wall. Forward, along the ship's longitudinal axis, there was a gap in the screen for the locator disc, almost twice the height of man in diameter. Transparent as crystal, the disc seemed to merge with cosmic space, sparkling like a black diamond in the light from the instrument dials.

Moot Ang made an almost imperceptible movement and all three at once threw up their arms to shield their eyes. A gigantic orange sun had burst out on the port side of the screen. Although

---

* Parsec is the unit of measurement of interstellar distances equal to 3.26 light years.

its intensity was reduced by powerful filters, the light was all but unbearable.

Moot Ang shook his head.

"We nearly went through the corona. No more exact courses laid out in advance for me! It's much safer to by-pass."

"The worst thing about these warp ships is that you lay the course and then shoot off blindly like a bullet fired into the night," Tey Eron's voice came from the depths of his seat. Tey was second in command and the head astrophysicist. "Besides, we too are blind and helpless cooped up inside the vortical protective fields. I don't like this kind of cosmic flight, even though it's the fastest way man has been able to devise."

"Twenty-four parsecs, yet to us it has seemed like an instant," Moot Ang said.

"An instant of death-like sleep," Tey Eron muttered gruffly. "As for the Earth...."

"It's best not to think about the Earth," Kari Ram said, getting up. "Or the fact that seventy-eight years have passed down there since we took off, or of the friends and folks at home who've died of old age, or the other changes. What will it be like when we get back I wonder?"

"It would be the same no matter what type of space ship you use," the captain said calmly. "The only difference is that in the *Tellur* time moves faster for us. Although we're going farther out into space than anybody before us, we'll be little changed when we return."

Tey Eron went over to the computer.

"Everything's normal," he said a few minutes later. "That's Cor Serpentis over there, or as the ancient Arab astronomers called it, Unuk al-Hay —the Heart of the Serpent."

"Where is its neighbour?" Kari Ram asked.

"Behind the main star. Look here: spectrum K-0. It's eclipsed for us."

"Strip all receptors!" ordered the captain.

The infinite blackness of the Cosmos enveloped everything—a bottomless blackness that seemed blacker still for the golden-orange blaze of Cor Serpentis port and aft. The Milky Way and other stars paled in the glare. Only one white star down below held its own.

"We're nearing Epsilon Serpentis," Kari Ram said. His voice was louder than necessary; he evidently expected a compliment from the captain. But Moot Ang said nothing. His eyes were turned to starboard, to the bright white blaze of the distant star.

'That's where my old ship, the *Sun*, went," he said at last, conscious of the expectant silence in the control room. "To explore new planets...."

"So that's Alphecca of the Corona Borealis!"

"Yes, Ram. Or to use its European name—Gemma. But it's time to get to work."

"Shall I wake the others?" Tey Eron asked.

"No. We'll make one or two warps if it's all clear ahead," Moot Ang said. "Switch on the optical and radio telescopes. Check the tuning of the memory machines. Tey, start the nuclear engines. We'll use them for the time being. Accelerate."

"Six-sevenths of the speed of light?"

The captain nodded and Tey quickly flipped over switches. Not a tremor passed through the space ship, only a blinding blaze lit up all the screens and completely blotted out the faint stars—our own Sun among them—of the Milky Way below.

"We have several hours to wait before the instruments complete the observations and check them over," Moot Ang said. "We'll eat now and then we had all better get some sleep. You carry on, Kari. I'll relieve you."

Kari Ram dropped into the swivel seat facing the centre of the control panel. When the two other men had gone, he switched off the stern receptors and the flames of the rocket engines disappeared from view.

The reflected glare of fiery Cor Serpentis danced on the gleaming surface of the instruments. The disc of the forward locator remained a black bottomless well. This was reassuring, for it showed that the calculations which had taken six years of work by the finest minds and computing machines on Earth were correct.

The *Tellur*, the first space-warp ship ever made on Earth, was moving down a great corridor in space devoid of stellar clusters and dark clouds. This type of ship, capable of moving in zero-space, was designed to reach much farther out into the Universe than the previous anameson nuclear-rocket ships which could not exceed five-sixths or six-sevenths of the speed of light. Operating on the principle of compression of time, warp ships were thousands of times faster. Their drawback was that during each lunge forward they were out of human control; as a matter of fact, astronauts could endure the moment of space warp only in an unconscious state, protected by a powerful vortical energy field. The *Tellur* moved in spurts, and before each spurt care had to be taken to see that the way ahead was clear.

Now the *Tellur* was on its way past the Serpent and through practically starless space in the high latitudes of the Galaxy to a carbon star in Hercules. The object of this incredibly distant journey was to study the still mysterious processes of transformation of matter directly on the carbon star. The findings would be of inestimable value to power development on Earth. There was a theory that the star itself had some connection with a disc-shaped electromagnetic dark cloud revolving edgewise to the Earth. Scientists thought the processes going on here in relative proximity to the Sun might be a repetition of the birth of our own planetary system, the "relative proximity" in this case meaning one hundred and ten parsecs, or three hundred and fifty light years.

Kari Ram checked the safety devices. They showed all the automatic installations of the ship to be working normally. He sat back and gave himself up to his thoughts.

The Earth was now far, far away. Seventy-eight light years separated them from the good and beautiful Earth which mankind had made a haven of happy life, of inspired, creative labour. In the classless society man had created for himself every individual knew his planet so well there was little left to learn—he knew not only its factories and mines and plantations, its marine industries and research centres, its museums and preserves, but also the quiet retreats where one could enjoy the beauties of Nature in solitude or with one's beloved.

It was a wonderful world, but man in his insatiable desire for more knowledge had reached out to the icy chasms of cosmic space, searching for the solution to the riddle of the Universe, eager to fathom Nature's secrets and subordinate her more and more to man's will. First he had reached the Moon and seen the lunar plains and mountains drenched in a lethal shower of X-ray and ultra-violet radiation from the Sun. Then on to torrid, lifeless Venus with its oceans of oil, sticky, tarry soil and eternal fog; on to cold, sandy Mars with only a faint flicker of life in its subterranean depths. Hardly had exploration of Jupiter begun when new ships reached the nearest stars. Space ships from Earth visited Alpha and Proxima Centauri, Barnard's star, Sirius, Eta Eridani and even Tau Ceti—not the stars themselves, but their planets or their immediate vicinities, as was the case with the twin stars of Sirius which have no planetary system.

But never had astronauts from Earth been on planets where life had reached its highest stage of development, in other words, planets inhabited by thinking beings.

From the infinity of the Cosmos ultrashort radio waves brought tidings of other populated worlds, sometimes reaching us thousands of years after they were sent out. Man was only learning to read these messages, obtaining the first inkling of the vast ocean of scientific and engineering skill and artistic accomplishment that washed the shores of the inhabited worlds of our Galaxy. These worlds were as yet beyond our reach. And what of those other worlds in island universes millions of light years away!

Knowledge of all this whetted man's eagerness to journey to planets inhabited by men—perhaps unlike our Earthmen, but men nevertheless who, like ourselves, had built rational, sane societies where every member had the right to his share of happiness in a measure limited only by the degree of mastery acquired over Nature. It had already been established that there existed worlds inhabited by people like ourselves, and that these were probably the majority. For the laws governing the development of planetary systems and of life on their planets were the same not only through our Galaxy, but throughout the entire known Universe.

The space-warp ship, the latest triumph of human genius, had made it possible to answer the call of all these distant worlds. And now the *Tellur* was on its way. If the flight was successful, then. . . . But as was the case with everything else in life, there was another side to this invention.

"Yes, there's the other side," Kari Ram said aloud, so completely immersed in his thoughts that he was unaware he had spoken until Moot

Ang's deep, resonant voice singing an old song brought him to with a start.

> *The other side of Love,*
> *Now rolling deep as the ocean's flood,*
> *Now narrow as a winding stair,*
> *There's no escape, 'tis in your blood,*

the captain sang.

"I had no idea you liked old songs too," he said. "That one's at least five hundred years old."

"I wasn't thinking about songs," replied the astronavigator. "I was thinking of this flight. And what Earth will be like when we return."

The captain's face clouded.

"We have only made the first warp. Are you already thinking of our return?"

"Oh no! You know how eager I was to be among the few chosen for the voyage. I was just thinking that when we return to Earth seven hundred years of terrestrial time will have passed. And even though the average life-span has doubled, our sisters' and brothers' great-grandchildren will be dead by then."

"Didn't you know that?"

"Of course. But something else has struck me."

"The seeming futility of our flight?"

"Exactly. Long before the *Tellur* was built or even invented, ordinary rocket ships set out for

Fomalhaut, Capella and Arcturus. That was fifty years ago, but the Fomalhaut expedition is expected back only two years from now. The Arcturus and Capella parties will be returning in some forty or fifty years; you know Arcturus is twelve and Capella fourteen parsecs away. But the warp ships being built now can get to Arcturus in one warp. The distance there is nothing in comparison with this flight. And by the time we get back people will have completely conquered time, or space, whichever way you want to put it. The space ships they will build then will have a range much greater than ours and leave us to waddle back with a cargo of obsolete and useless information."

"You mean our departure from Earth was something like death, and that we'll return as primitive men, mere survivals of an age long past?" Moot Ang said.

"Yes."

"You're right and at the same time completely wrong. Accumulation of knowledge and experience, including exploration of the Universe, must never cease. Otherwise the laws of development would be violated, and development is always uneven and contradictory. Suppose the ancient scientists who now seem naive to us had waited for, say, the modern quantum microscope to be invented. Or if the farmers and builders of ancient times who drenched the earth with their sweat had decided to do nothing before automatic machines were made. Had they done that we would still be living in holes in the ground and subsisting on the crumbs Nature might bestow on us."

Kari Ram laughed, but Moot Ang went on.

"Besides, we have our duty to perform, like every other member of society. The price of being the first to penetrate to hitherto inaccessible parts of the Universe is to die for seven hundred years. But those who remained behind to enjoy all the pleasures of terrestrial life will never know the wonder and joy of glimpsing the innermost secrets of the Universe. As for going back ... I don't think you need to fear the future. There has never been an age since the beginning of human history when mankind did not retain something of the past in spite of the ascending spiral of progress. Every century has had, besides its own unique peculiarities, features common to all times. Who knows but that the tiny particle of knowledge we shall take back to Earth will help to bring about a new advance in science, to make men's lives still richer and fuller. And even if we ourselves will be returning from the distant past, are our lives not dedicated to the future? Can we be strangers to the new people we shall be going to? In general, can anyone who gives his all to society be a stranger to his fellow-men? You must admit that man is more than just an accumulation of knowledge; he is also a carrier of complex emotions, and in this respect we shall not be found wanting after the trials of our voyage." He paused, then added in a lighter tone: "Speaking for myself, I am so eager to look into the future that for that alone...."

"You're ready to die for a while as far as the Earth is concerned?" prompted the navigator.

The captain nodded.

"You'd better go and have something to eat," he said. "It'll soon be time for the next warp. What are you doing here, Tey?"

The second-in-command shrugged his shoulders.

"I wanted to take a look at the course the instruments have plotted. And it's time to relieve you."

He pressed a button in the centre of the panel and a polished concave cover slid open. A spiral of silver-coloured metal ribbon rose from the depths of the instrument. Through it ran a black needle indicating the course of the ship. Tiny lights gleaming like jewels on the spiral represented the stars of various spectral classes past which the *Tellur*'s course lay. On innumerable dials indicator needles danced as the computing machines worked out the direction of the next warp so as to keep the ship well away from the stars and dark clouds and luminous nebulae that might conceal unknown heavenly bodies.

Tey Eron was so engrossed in his task that he hardly noticed the passage of time. In the meantime the huge space ship continued hurtling through the black emptiness of the Cosmos. While the astrophysicist worked, his two comrades sat in silence in the soft depths of a semi-circular seat just inside the massive triple door that separated the control room from the rest of the ship.

Several hours later a gay tinkle of chimes announced that the computations were finished. The captain walked over to the control panel.

"Excellent! The next warp can be nearly three times as long as the first."

"Not as much as that. Look at this...." Tey pointed to the tip of the black needle which was vibrating faintly in rhythm with a series of indicators.

"At any rate fifty-seven parsecs gives complete certainty. Knock off five to allow a margin of error. That leaves fifty-two. Stand by for the warp."

Again the countless devices and relays were checked over. Moot Ang plugged in on the cabins where the remaining five crew members were fast asleep.

The automatic physiological observation devices reported all five in normal condition. This established, the captain switched on the protective field around the crew's quarters. Red streaks running along the frosted paneling on the port wall showed the flow of gas through the tubes concealed behind.

"Ready?" Tey Eron asked the commander.

The captain nodded, and the three men in the navigation room settled into their deep padded seats. Secured firmly with air cushions, each took a metal hypodermic syringe ready for use from a compartment in the left arm rest.

"Well, here goes—for another hundred and fifty years of Earth-life," said Kari Ram, driving the point of the needle into his arm.

Moot Ang looked at him sharply. But the faintly mocking gleam in the young man's eyes reassured him. When his comrades had dropped back in their seats and lost consciousness, the captain switched on the robots controlling both the warp mechanism and the protective shield, and finally flipped over some levers on a small box next to his knee which brought the massive domes down noiselessly from the ceiling. When the domes were in place, he took one last glance at the dials now illuminated with a dim bluish light and plunged the hypodermic needle into his arm.

* * *

The ship came out of its fourth warp. It was cruising along at a speed less than that of light not quite four parsecs away from its destination—the dark giant KNT8008 belonging to the rare class of dark carbon stars. The most powerful telescopes on Earth could hardly pick it out, but now it loomed as large as the Sun viewed from Mercury on the starboard, or "north," screens of the ship.

Stars like this with diameters 150 to 170 times the diameter of the Sun were distinguished by the abundance of carbon in their atmospheres. At a temperature of 2,000-3,000°C. the carbon atoms formed a specific type of molecules consisting of three atoms each. Stellar atmospheres with such a molecular structure absorbed radiation in the violet region of the spectrum and hence the luminosity of stars of this class was very low in relation to their size.

The cores of the carbon giants, however, had temperatures running to 100 million degrees, and this made them powerful neutron generators that transformed light elements into heavy ones, even heavier than uranium, all the way to californium and rossium. The latter was the heaviest of the known elements, with an atomic weight of 401, and had first been obtained a good four centuries earlier.

Scientists believed it was the carbon stars that were the Universe's factories of heavy elements which they spread into space in periodical eruptions, and that they were the source of the new chemical elements that were constantly appearing in our Galaxy. The advent of the warp ship now enabled man to study carbon stars at close range, and observe the processes of transformation of matter going on there.

The crew of the *Tellur* had regained consciousness and were at work on the research programme for the sake of which they had cut themselves off from Earth for seven hundred terrestrial years. All were fully aware that they had a long job ahead of them. The processes the expedition was to investigate were complex indeed and physicists on Earth had not yet been able to find a clue to their secrets.

The ship seemed to be cruising very slowly now, but no greater speed was needed. Its course deviated somewhat to the south from a straight line to the carbon star so as to keep the locator screen shaded from its radiation; indeed the disc remained a black void for weeks and months and years in succession.

The *Tellur*, or *IF-1 (Z-685)*, as it was listed in the register of the Earth's Cosmic fleet (meaning the first inverted-field space ship, and the 685th ever to be built), was not as huge as the long-range subphotonic space ships which had preceded it. The older type of ship had carried crews of up to two hundred, and their voyages had lasted the lifetime of more than one generation, which enabled them to penetrate quite deep into interstellar space. Each time one of these long-range ships returned, however, it brought back with it several score men and women from the distant past. But while physiologically and intellectually on a high level of development, they found it so hard to adapt themselves to the times that many of them succumbed to melancholy and depression.

Now warp ships would carry people still farther out into the Cosmos, and in a very short time— as time is measured by astronauts—Methuselahs a thousand years old would be appearing in human society. Those who would undertake voyages to other island universes would be returning to their native planet millions of years later. This was the negative side of cosmic exploration —the great barrier Nature had laid in the path of the cosmic ambitions of her restless Earthsons.

The latest space ships carried a crew of only eight. And whereas previously astronauts had been encouraged to raise families during flights, these travellers into boundless space and the future were strictly forbidden to do so.

Although the *Tellur* was smaller than its predecessors, its dimensions were nevertheless huge for so small a crew.

As always after a long sleep, the eight astronauts on board, most of them young people, were brimming with energy that sought an outlet, and they spent most of their free time in the gymnasium. They devised all sorts of difficult exercises and complicated dances, or performed the most fantastic acrobatics in the antigravitation corner of the hall. Another favourite pastime was swimming in the big pool filled with ionized luminescent water that retained the exquisite blue of that cradle of humanity, the Mediterranean.

Kari Ram was hurrying to the swimming pool when he heard a melodious voice behind him.

"I need your help, Kari. This turn just won't come off right."

The speaker was Taina Dan, a tall, slender girl in a short tunic of a shining green fabric that matched her eyes. She was the party's chemist, the youngest and most high-spirited member of the expedition. Often enough she irritated the staid, level-headed Kari by her impulsiveness, but he shared her passion for dancing. Smiling, he turned and went toward her.

Afra Devi, the expedition's biologist, called out to him from the diving board as he passed by. With her back to the water, she was pulling a bathing cap over her luxurious black hair. In the meantime Tey Eron came up to Afra on the springy plastic diving board and held out his muscular arm behind the girl's back. She threw herself backward against Tey's arm and for a fraction of a second was balanced there, then completed the turn around the arm and the two plunged down into the water, their tawny skins gleaming with that glint of bronze that only a healthy outdoor life can give. Kari's eyes followed them.

"He's forgotten all about me!" Taina cried, pressing the tips of her fingers against his eyes.

"But it was beautiful, wasn't it?" Kari replied, drawing the girl to him and leading her into the first step of the dance as they entered the sound strip.

Kari and Taina were the best dancers on board. None of the others could abandon themselves so completely to melody and rhythm. Now too Kari was swept into the world of dance, oblivious to everything but the fascination of co-ordinated movement. The girl's hand resting on his shoulder was at once strong and tender. Her green eyes deepened in colour.

"You are just like your name," Kari whispered. "I believe in an ancient language 'Taina' meant something mysterious, unfathomed."

"I'm glad of that," the girl replied gravely. "I had thought that the mysterious and unfathomed existed only in the Cosmos—that it didn't apply to Earth any more. It certainly doesn't to people—there's nothing enigmatic or unpredictable about us."

"Do you regret it?"

"Sometimes. I should like to meet someone like the people who lived in the distant past. Someone who has to hide his dreams and his feelings from a hostile environment, to steel his resolve in secret and to build up his will till nothing can shake it."

"I see what you mean. But I wasn't thinking of people—only of unfathomed secrets.... The kind one reads about in ancient novels—mysterious ruins, unknown depths, unattained heights. And before that there were enchanted forests and springs and haunted houses where all sorts of exciting supernatural things happened."

"Wouldn't it be wonderful, Kari, to find some secret passage on board...."

"Leading to some mysterious chambers where...."

"Yes, Kari, go on."

"My imagination doesn't go any further," said the engineer.

But Taina had got into the spirit of the thing and she pulled Kari after her into a dimly-lit side passage. The vibration indicators blinked wearily on the walls as if the ship itself was fighting an overpowering drowsiness. Taina tiptoed down the corridor a little way and then stopped. A shadow of boredom flitted over her face but was gone before Kari could be certain that he had really seen it. An unfamiliar emotion seized him and he took the girl's hand again.

"Let's go to the library," he said. "I've still got two hours before my watch."

She followed him obediently.

The library was a large common room with indirect lighting that created the illusion of a luminous mist floating under the ceiling. It was located immediately aft of the central control room, as was customary in all space ships. Kari and Taina opened the pressurized door of the third transverse passage and came to the double-doored elliptical hatchway of the central gallery,

No sooner had Kari stepped on the bronze plate in front of it and caused the heavy leaves to slide open than the air grew vibrant with sound. Taina brightened.

"It's Moot Ang," she said, pressing Kari's fingers.

They slipped into the library. There were three men in the room. The ship's doctor, Svet Sim, and the stocky warp engineer Yas Tin, were ensconced in soft armchairs between the upright columns of the film cabinets, and to the left, the commander of the *Tellur* himself was bent over the keys of the EMV.

The EMV, or electromagnetic viono, had long replaced the harsh-toned piano of old, retaining the tonal wealth of the piano but imparting to it the melodious richness of the violin. Amplifiers could give the sounds it produced an amazing power.

Moot Ang was unaware of the newcomers. He sat, leaning forward slightly, his face lifted to the rhombic panels of the ceiling, his fingers running lightly over the keyboard. As in the old-time piano, every nuance of sound depended on the musician's touch, although the sound itself was produced not by hammers striking strings but by delicate electronic impulses that might almost be compared to the nerve impulses of the human brain.

The music flowed in interweaving harmonies that spoke of the fusion of Earth and Cosmos. Presently the pattern broke, notes of wistful melancholy mingled with the rumble of a distant storm in a gradual crescendo of sound through which rang notes like cries of despair. The tension rose higher and higher until it reached the final cataclysmic burst that resolved itself in an avalanche of dissonances sliding down and down into a dark abyss of inconsolable grief for that which was gone for ever.

But suddenly pure clear notes of limpid joy rang out under Moot Ang's fingers and merged with the gentle sadness of the accompaniment.

Just then the door opened and Afra Devi, who had changed into a white smock, slipped into the room and went over to Svet Sim. The doctor listened to her, then signed to the captain. The captain's hands left the keyboard and silence broke the spell of the music as swiftly as the tropical night banishes day.

The captain left the room with the doctor followed by the worried glances of the others. Something most unusual had occurred—the second navigator had had an attack of acute appendicitis. He had evidently neglected to carry out the full programme of medical preparation for the voyage. Now Dr. Sim had to ask the captain's permission to operate without delay.

Moot Ang hesitated. Modern medicine, with its methods of regulating nervous activity in much the same way as the impulses were regulated in electronic devices, was able to cure a great many ailments. But the doctor insisted. He argued that although the condition could be cured at the moment, the enormous strain imposed on the organism by cosmic flight might cause a relapse.

The patient was placed on a wide operating table and enmeshed in a maze of wires leading to the thirty-six electronic devices that gave a complete picture of his condition. The hypnotic sleep-inducer blinked and hummed rhythmically in the darkened room. Dr. Sim read the instruments once more and nodded to Afra Devi. It was her job to assist the doctor. Each member of the crew, besides being an expert in some branch of science, was trained for some particular shipboard duty—servicing the ship's mechanisms, taking care of the feeding arrangements, and so on.

Afra brought out a transparent vessel filled with a bluish liquid. In it lay a segmented metal device resembling a good-sized centipede. Afra took out the device and from another vessel she extracted a conical-shaped instrument attached to some long fine tubes. A light click and the metallic centipede came to life with a barely audible whirr.

Svet Sim nodded and the apparatus was inserted in the patient's mouth. Moot Ang moved closer to the semitransparent screen which had been placed at an angle over the sick man's abdomen. In the greenish glow of the screen the grey contours of the internal organs and the segmented metal device making its way down the alimentary canal were clearly visible. In a little while its blunt end was pressed against the base of the appendix.

With the apparatus pressing in the area of inflammation the pain increased and sedatives had to be administered to counteract the convulsions that appeared in the intestines. In a few minutes the data processor had completed the diagnosis and recommended the antibiotics and disinfectants needed. The metallic centipede inserted its long flexible feelers deep into the appendix and sucked out the pus and the alien bodies that had caused the inflammatory process. This was followed by a vigorous irrigation with biological solutions which quickly restored the mucous membranes of the appendix and the adjoining intestine to normal.

The patient slept peacefully while the ingenious automatic device did its work. Now the operation was over and it only remained for the doctor to remove the instrument.

The captain heaved a sigh of relief. Despite the power of medicine, unforeseen peculiarities of individual organisms often resulted in unexpected complications, for it was obviously impossible to establish in advance every deviation from the normal among all the thousands of millions of inhabitants of the Earth. And if these possible complications were nothing to worry about on Earth with its great medical institutions, they could very well be dangerous enough on expeditions like the present.

But everything had gone off well. With an easy mind Moot Ang returned to the now deserted library and sat down at the viono. But he did not play, though his hands rested on the keys. Instead his thoughts returned, as they had so many times before, to human happiness and the future.

This was his fourth voyage into the Cosmos. But never before had he embarked on a flight covering so much space and time. With man forging ahead at great speed from one accomplishment and discovery to another, with the sum total of knowledge mankind had accumulated, seven hundred years now could hardly be compared with an equal span of Earth-time in the days of the ancient civilizations. Then society's progress was limited to opening up formerly uninhabited expanses of our planet to human habitation. In those distant days, time crawled and human progress was as slow as the movement of the Arctic and Antarctic glaciers. Time seemed to have stood still for centuries. What indeed did the human life-span amount to then, or a century, or ten centuries, for that matter?

What would the people of the ancient world have felt, Moot Ang thought with a shudder, had they known in advance how slow social development would be, had they foreseen that oppression, injustice and chaos were to remain man's lot for so many years to come? You could sleep for seven hundred years in ancient Egypt and wake up to find the same slave system in existence, except for perhaps even more brutal exploitation. In ancient China seven-hundred-year spans began and ended with the same wars, the same dynasties, and Europe passed in like time only from the beginning of the Dark Ages to the height of the Inquisition.

But now the mere thought of the grand vistas that would be opened up by the next seven centuries—centuries packed with changes, improvements in life, ever new knowledge—staggered the imagination.

And if true happiness consists in movement, change, rapid progress, Moot Ang mused, who could be happier than he and his comrades? Yet things are not as simple as they might seem. Man's nature is as complex as his environment. While reaching ever forward, we are always saddened by the passage of time, or rather by the loss of the fine things of the past—things that are hallowed by memory and that once gave rise to legends about golden ages vanished in the labyrinths of time.

Men could not help looking to whatever had been good in the past, and yearning for its return, for only the most clear-minded were able to foresee the inevitable coming of something better in the future. And ever since then there has persisted in the minds of men a deep regret for that which is gone, a nostalgic longing for what has ceased to be, a sadness one most poignantly feels when viewing ancient ruins and monuments to mankind's past history. One felt all this more and more keenly as one grew older.

Moot Ang rose from his seat and squared his powerful shoulders.

Yes, all that had been vividly described in historical novels. But what was there to frighten the young men and women on board a space ship bound for the future? Loneliness? The loss of one's relatives? The loneliness of a man projected into the future had often been described in old novels. It had meant being torn away from one's kin. Yet these kinsfolk had been a handful of individuals linked only by the formal bond of blood. Were not all men brothers now, had not the old conventions and barriers between men everywhere on Earth been banished for ever?

What should he, the captain of the *Tellur*, tell his young colleagues? "We of the *Tellur* have lost all those whom we hold near and dear on Earth. But the people awaiting us in the future are no less near and dear to us—their minds will be keener and their feelings richer than those of the contemporaries we have left behind...." Yes, that is what he must tell them.

In the meanwhile Tey Eron was at work in the control room. As usual, he had turned off all the unnecessary lights and in the half-gloom the large round chamber looked cosier. Humming a simple tune, he was checking the calculations over and over again. The ship was nearing the farthest point on its journey, and today the course would have to be altered in the direction of Serpentarius in order to skirt the carbon star they were investigating. But it was still dangerous to approach it. The increasing pressure of its radiation was apt to wreck the ship moving at a speed close to that of light.

Sensing someone behind him, Tey Eron turned to face his commander.

Moot Ang leaned over his assistant's shoulder to scan the summarized indicator readings flashed on in a row of little square windows along the lower edge of the control panel. Tey Eron looked up at him questioningly. The captain nodded. In response to a barely perceptible movement of Tey Eron's fingers the intercommunication system sprang into action. There was a pealing of bells through the ship accompanied by the metallic words: "Attention all!"

Moot Ang pulled the microphone toward himself, knowing that all members of the crew were tensely waiting for the next words to come from the loudspeakers concealed in the walls.

"Attention all!" Moot Ang repeated. "Deceleration in fifteen minutes. All except those on duty should lie down in their cabins. The first phase of deceleration will end at 18:00 hours, the second phase at 6g will continue for 144 hours. Change in course after Collision Danger signal. That's all!"

At 18:00 hours the captain rose from his seat, conscious of the usual deceleration pains in his back and the back of his head, and announced that he would retire to his cabin for the remaining six days of braking action ahead. The rest of the crew sat glued to their instruments for this was their last opportunity to observe the carbon star.

Tey Eron frowned as he watched the captain leave the control room. He would have felt better with the captain there beside him during the difficult manoeuvre. For although there was little comparison between a powerful cosmic ship like the *Tellur* and those flimsy shells called ships that plied the Earth's seas, it too was nothing more than an egg-shell in the infinity of space.

* * *

Kari Ram started at the sound of Moot Ang's merry laugh. A few days ago the crew had been greatly alarmed to learn that the captain had been suddenly taken ill. Only the doctor had been allowed to enter his cabin, and everyone had spoken in whispers when passing the tightly-closed door. With the captain laid up the task of bringing the ship around and accelerating again to get it away from the radiation zone of the carbon star and send it back toward the Sun and home had been left to Tey Eron.

Now Tey Eron was walking beside the captain

with a faint smile on his lips. He had just learned that the latter had conspired with the doctor to leave the ship in Tey's hands and force him to rely on himself alone. He would not confess to the agonized doubts that had assailed him just before he swung the ship around, but he reproached the captain for having unnecessarily alarmed the crew.

Moot Ang laughed it all off and assured Tey that the ship was perfectly safe in the great open spaces of the Cosmos. The instruments could not err, and the system of fourfold check-up of every computation excluded the possibility of mistakes. Nor could there be any belt of asteroids and meteorites in the vicinity of the carbon star: the pressure of radiation was too heavy.

"You really think there will be no more surprises?" Kari Ram put in cautiously.

"Unforeseen accidents, of course, are always possible. But that great law of the Cosmos we call the law of averages works in our favour. You can be certain that in this deserted corner of the Universe we cannot expect to run into anything new. We shall go back some distance and warp back along our old path to the Sun, past the Heart of the Serpent. For some days now we've been heading for Serpentarius. We'll be there soon enough."

"Strange, but I feel no joy, no satisfaction at a job well done, nothing that might justify leaving Earth-life for seven hundred years," Kari went on thoughtfully. "Oh yes, I know all about the tens of thousands of observations and millions of computations, photographs and notes—all that will help to delve deeper into the secrets of matter back on Earth.... But how inconsequential it all seems! A mere spore of the future—nothing more."

"Have you ever stopped to think of the effort humanity has spent and the lives it has sacrificed for the sake of what you call spores of the future —not to speak of the countless generations of unthinking animals that preceded it on the ladder of historical progress?" Tey Eron said heatedly.

"You're right enough, so far as reason goes. But emotionally the only thing that matters for me is Man, the only rational force in the Universe, capable of mastering and making use of the elemental development of matter. Yet how infinite is Man's solitude! We know beyond doubt that there are many inhabited worlds, but Earthmen have not yet met another thinking being in all the vastness of space. Do you realize how long men have dreamed—in vain—of such encounters, how many books have been written, how many songs composed and pictures painted in anticipation of the great event? And yet this dream cherished ever since religious blindness first began to be dispelled has not yet come true."

"You speak of blindness," Moot Ang put in. "Do you know how our distant forebears back at the time of the Initial Emergence in Space visualized encounters with the inhabitants of other worlds? War, destruction of each other's ships, mutual killing at the very first encounter."

"Incredible!" Kari Ram and Tey Eron cried in one voice.

"Our modern writers seem to have preferred not to write about the period of the decline of capitalism," Moot Ang went on. "But you know from your school history books about that critical period in human development."

"Of course," Kari said. "Though man had begun to master matter and space, social relations retained their old forms and the development of social thought lagged behind the achievements of science."

"You have a good memory, Kari. But we could put it this way too: man's conquest of space, his knowledge of the Universe, clashed with the primitive thinking of the individualistic property-owner. The future and the very life of humanity hung in the balance for years before progress triumphed and mankind joined into one family in a classless society. Before that happened people in the capitalist half of the world refused for a long time to see any new paths into the future and regarded their mode of life as eternal and unchanging, with war and self-destruction as man's inevitable lot."

"Most likely, every civilization has its critical periods in whatever planet and solar system it may exist," Tey Eron said, running a quick eye over the instrument panel. "So far we've found two planets where there is water and an atmosphere with traces of oxygen, but no sign of life. We've photographed lifeless wind-swept sands and dead seas and...."

"I just can't believe it," Kari Ram interrupted him, "I can't believe that people who had already savoured the infinity of space and the power that science gave them could...."

"... reason like beasts who have just acquired the faculty of logical thinking?" Moot Ang completed his thought. "Don't forget the old society came into being as a result of an elemental play of forces, without the planning and foresight which distinguish the higher social forms created by man. Man's thinking, the very nature of his reasoning, was still at the primitive stage of simple, mathematical logic, which reflected the logic of the laws governing the development of matter and nature as perceived through direct observation. But as soon as mankind accumulated enough historical experience and came to perceive the whole historical process of the development of the world around it, dialectical logic appeared as the highest stage of thought. Man came to understand the duality of the phenomena of nature and his own existence. He realized that while as an individual he was as minute and transitory as a drop of water in the ocean or a spark struck in a high wind, he was at the same time as great as the Universe which his reason and emotions embraced in the infinity of time and space."

The captain rose and paced back and forth in silence while the others watched in deep concentration. Then he continued:

"I happen to have in my film library a book that gives an excellent picture of that time. It was translated into Modern not by machine, but by Sania Chen, the last-century historian. I think we ought to read it."

The young people were eager to start at once. Pleased at their reaction, Moot Ang left the control room to fetch the book.

"I know I'll never make a real captain," Tey Eron sighed. "I'll never know as much as Ang."

"I heard him say once that his biggest shortcoming is the wide range of his interests," Kari put in as he settled down in the navigator's seat.

Tey Eron looked at Kari in wonder. Neither spoke and the room was soundless except for the even hum of the navigation instruments. The ship was running at full speed away from the carbon star toward a quarter of the Universe where four island universes quivered in the blackness of space as pinpricks of light too tiny to be detected by the naked eye.

Suddenly a glowing spot burst out and trembled on the main locator screen and the pealing of the caution signal cut through the control room. For a moment the men in the room froze into breathless immobility.

Then Tey Eron gave the alarm signal that sent every member of the crew to his post.

Moot Ang rushed into the control room and in one bound was at the control panel. The black screen of the locator was no longer dead; on it, as in a bottomless lake, swam a tiny glowing globe with sharply defined outline, swaying up and down but slowly bearing to starboard. The robots on guard against collision with meteorites did not react, however. Did this mean that the spot of light on the screen was a reflection not of their own beam, but of someone else's?

The ship was still following the same course

and the spot of light was now quivering in the bottom starboard square of the screen. Realization of what this meant made the three men quiver with excitement. Kari Ram gripped the edge of the control panel until his hands hurt. Something stupendous and unimaginable was coming toward them preceded by a powerful locator ray of the kind the *Tellur* cast ahead.

So great was the captain's hope that his surmise should prove correct, and so great his fear that this upsurge of hope might again end in the bitter disappointment Earth astronauts had experienced hundreds of times before, that for a moment he could not speak.

The spot of light on the screen went out, came on again, then flashed on and off at regular intervals—four quick flashes, a pause, then two in succession. Such a patern of regularity could be attributed only to human agency—the sole rational force in the Universe.

There could be no doubt now—another space ship was heading toward them. And in these parts of the Universe where ships from the Earth had never been before it could only be a ship from another world, from some planet of another, distant sun.

The locator of the *Tellur* too was now sending out intermittent signals; the thought that they were probably being received on board the unknown ship seemed utterly fantastic.

Moot Ang's voice coming over the intercommunication system betrayed his agitation:

"Attention all! An unknown ship is approaching. We shall veer off course and begin emergency deceleration. All hands to landing stations!"

There wasn't a second to lose. If the oncoming ship was running at roughly the same speed as the *Tellur*, the two were approaching each other almost at the speed of light, or some 294,000 kilometres per second. According to the locator the gap would close in no more than one hundred seconds. While Moot Ang was at the microphone, Tey Eron whispered something to Kari, whose hand flew to the locator panel.

"Excellent!" cried the captain as he watched the light ray playing on the control screen describe a curve to port and then go into a spiral.

In some ten seconds a glowing arrow-like shape appeared on the screen, curved over the right side of the black circle and also went into a spiral. A sigh of relief that was more like a groan broke from the three men in the control room. The strangers coming towards them from the unfathomed depths of the Cosmos had understood them. Just in time!

The caution signal went on again. This time it

was not a locator ray but the solid hull of a space ship that was reflected on the main screen. In an instant Tey Eron had switched off the robot and turned the ship a fraction to port. The pealing stopped and the main screen was black again. The starboard scanner showed a mere streak of light moving aft. The two ships had passed each other at a staggering speed and were now hurtling farther and farther apart.

Several days would pass before they could meet again, but meet they would, for like the *Tellur* the strange ship would brake and swing around and return to the point of their meeting as determined by the precision instruments on board.

"Attention all! Emergency deceleration! All stations signal readiness!" Moot Ang spoke into the microphone.

In response the row of lights above the now dead engine counter indicators turned green one after the other. The engines had stopped, and a tense air of expectation settled over the ship. The captain glanced quickly at the control panel and nodded toward the seats as he switched on the deceleration robot. His aides saw him bend grim-faced over the programme scale and turn the main switch to the figure "8."

To swallow a pill to reduce heart action, drop

into the seat and press the robot button was a matter of seconds.

The ship seemed to brace itself against the emptiness of space, throwing its crew into the depths of hydraulic seats and momentary unconsciousness, just as the racehorses of old would throw their riders as they dug their hooves into the ground to come to a sudden stop.

* * *

The crew of the *Tellur* had gathered in the library. Everybody was there except the man on duty at the electronic devices control post designed to signalize if anything went wrong with any of the circuits. The ship had cut its speed enough to put about, but not before it had travelled more than ten thousand million kilometres beyond the point where it had passed the space ship from another world. It was now moving at only one-twentieth absolute speed, held to the exact return course by the computing devices. At least eight terrestrial days would pass before the two ships could be expected to meet—provided the *Tellur* kept within the margin of error allowed for and the unknown space travellers also possessed equally precise navigation instruments and an equally reliable ship. If everything went well the two ships, two tiny specks in the infinity of the

Cosmos, might be expected to come within locator range of each other.

When that happened, man, for the first time in his history, would meet his counterparts from another part of the Universe, thinking beings with comparable powers and aspirations whose existence had been foretold and established beyond all doubt by human reason. If hitherto the vast gulfs of time and space that separated different inhabited worlds had been insurmountable, now Earthmen would clasp the hands of other thinking beings and establish through them a link with still others as a token of the final triumph of thought and conscious labour over the elemental forces of Nature.

For billions of years minute droplets of living protoplasm had inhabited the dark warm waters of ocean gulfs, and hundreds of millions of years more passed before they developed into more complex organisms that finally emerged from the water to dry land. Then more millions of centuries passed in an elemental struggle for survival, in complete dependence on the forces of Nature, before the brain developed into a powerful instrument to guide the living creatures' search for food and the battle they waged for survival.

The rate of development speeded up, the battle to exist grew more bitter and natural selection proceeded at an ever more rapid pace. And all along that long path there were countless victims —herbivorous animals devoured by carnivorous, carnivorous animals that perished from hunger, the weak and sick and old that succumbed, the males that were killed in battle over females, those that perished defending their young or in natural disasters....

This went on through the long course of blind, elemental evolution until some distant relative of the ape in the rigorous conditions of the great ice age replaced instinct with conscious labour in his search for sustenance. It was then that he became man after he first realized the mighty power of joint labour and rational experience.

But even after this thousands of years were still to pass in wars and suffering, hunger and oppression and ignorance; but always too there dwelt hope and faith in a better future.

That hope and faith were not betrayed. The radiant future men had looked forward to had come, and humanity, united in a classless society and free of fear and oppression, had reached heights of scientific and artistic achievement without equal in all previous history. What had seemed the most difficult of all—the conquest of space—was accomplished. And finally, as the culmination of this long and laborious ascent up the ladder of progress, the latest fruit of man's accumulated knowledge and labour—the invention of the *Tellur*, this long-range space ship now exploring remote areas of the Universe. Now this supreme product of the development of matter on Earth and in the Solar System was about to contact what represented the crowning accomplishment of another, and probably no less tortuous and difficult, path of development that started thousands of millions of years ago in another corner of the Universe.

These were the thoughts that in one form or another occupied the minds of all the members of the *Tellur* crew. Even young Taina was awed by the tremendous significance of the moment. Would they, a handful of people representing all the thousands of millions inhabiting the Earth, prove worthy of their exploits in labour, their physical perfection, their intelligence and steadfastness? How was one to prepare oneself for the meeting? There was no better way than to review the great yet bitter battle humanity had waged for freedom of body and spirit.

At the moment, however, most exciting was the thought of the coming meeting with living creatures from another world. What would they be like? Monsters, or models of perfection, judged by Earth standards?

Afra Devi, the biologist, was the first to speak.

Flushed with excitement, she looked even more beautiful than usual. As she spoke her glance rested from time to time on the painting over the door—a coloured panorama in three-dimensional paint of a mountain scene in Equatorial Africa. The startling contrast between the sombre, forest-clad slopes and the shining splendour of the peak seemed to illustrate her thoughts.

Afra recalled the time long ago when it was still widely believed that thinking beings could exist in practically any form, that the structure of their organisms could vary greatly. That was when the survivals of religious prejudices induced even serious scientists to assume that a brain could develop in any body—just as men once believed gods could assume any physical form. Actually, however, the anatomy and physiology of man, the only creature with a brain capable of rational thinking on Earth, were not the result of some accidental caprice of Nature. On the contrary, they represented a maximum degree of adaptation to environment and corresponded to man's highly developed reasoning powers and nervous activity.

Our concepts of beauty in human beings and beauty in general evolved in the course of thousands of years as a result of unconscious acceptance of structural expediency and forms best adapted for one action or another. That is why we see beauty in powerful machines, in ocean waves, in trees and in horses, although none of these have anything in common with beauty as we see it in human beings. Even at the animal stage, man, thanks to the development of his brain, ceased to be compelled to adapt himself to only one mode of life as is the case with most animals.

Human legs are not adapted for constant running even on firm ground, yet they enable man to travel far and fast and to climb trees and rocks. As for the human hand, it is the most universal organ, capable of doing millions of things; indeed it was the hand that transformed the primitive beast into a human being....

In other words, man beginning with the earliest stages of his development evolved as a universal organism adapted to a great variety of conditions. With subsequent socialization of his existence, man's organism became increasingly adapted to his multiform activities. As distinct from all other animals, the beauty of human beings consists, besides physical perfection, in their universality enhanced by the activity of the mind and nobility of spirit.

"Any thinking being from some other world

that has been able to reach the Cosmos must be just as perfect and universal as the humans of our Earth, and hence just as beautiful," Afra went on. "There can be no thinking monsters, no mushroom-men, no octopus-men! I cannot say what we shall meet in reality—some similarity of form or other aspect of beauty, but that it will be beauty, I have no doubt."

"I like your theory," Tey Eron said. "But...."

"I know what you mean," Afra cut in. "Even slight departures from the norm can produce monstrosities, and here departures are highly probable. A human face without a nose, eyelids or lips is repulsive because the disfigurement is a departure from the normal. The face of a horse or dog also differs greatly from the human face, but we do not consider it ugly. On the contrary, it can be beautiful. The reason for this is that its beauty springs from natural expediency, whereas in the disfigured human face natural harmony has been upset."

"You suggest that even if they may look quite different from us, we may not think them ugly?" Tey persisted. "But supposing they resemble us but have horns and elephant-like trunks?"

"A thinking being does not need horns and hence will not have them. The nose may be somewhat elongated to form a trunk, although a trunk too is unnecessary for a being with hands, and a human being must have hands. If there is a trunk, it will be a mere exception to the rule. But everything that comes into being as a result of historical development, of natural selection becomes the rule, however numerous the exceptions. Therein lies the beauty of expediency. No, I do not expect to find monsters with horns and tails in the space ship we shall meet. Only the lower forms of life differ greatly from one another; the higher the form the closer it is bound to be to us Earth-dwellers."

"You win," Tey Eron said, looking around at the others with obvious pride in Afra's logic.

Kari Ram held another view, however, and he propounded it in his somewhat diffident manner. He believed that the strange beings, even if they were quite human in appearance and beautiful besides, might prove to be utterly remote from us as regards intelligence and outlook on life. In which case they might turn out to be cruel and terrible enemies.

Moot Ang came to the defence of the biologist.

"I happened to think of this quite recently," he said. "And I realized that at the highest stage of development all thinking beings must reach a state of perfect mutual understanding. The mind of the intelligent being reflects the laws governing the development of the entire Universe. In this sense man is a microcosm. Thinking follows the laws of the Universe which are the same everywhere. Thought, no matter where it is found, will inevitably be based on mathematical and dialectical logic. There cannot be any other entirely different thought process, just as man cannot exist outside of society and Nature...."

A murmur of approval rose from his listeners.

"How wonderful it is when the ideas of many people coincide!" said Afra Devi. "That is proof of their correctness and evidence of a sense of comradeship ... especially if each approaches a problem from the standpoint of his own particular branch of learning."

"You mean biology and the social sciences?" asked Yas Tin who had taken no part in the conversation so far.

"Yes. The brightest page in the entire history of man on Earth was the steady growth of mutual understanding that accompanied the development of culture and knowledge. The higher the level of culture, the easier it was for the different peoples and races in the classless society to understand one another, and the clearer became the common goals of human existence, the need to unite first countries and then the whole planet. At the present level of development attained by humanity on Earth and no doubt by those we are about to meet...." Afra broke off.

"Yes, indeed," agreed Moot Ang. "Two different planets meeting in outer space will be able to understand each other better than two savage nations on a single planet!"

"But what about the theory that war is inevitable even in the Cosmos?" asked Kari Ram. "Our ancestors who already were at a rather high level of culture were convinced of it."

"Where is that book you promised to show us?" Tey Eron remembered. "The one about the two space ships which tried to destroy each other at their first meeting?"

The commander went to his room. This time nothing interfered and he returned shortly carrying the small eight-rayed star of a microfilm roll which he placed in the reading machine. The astronauts gathered around to hear the tale of fantasy told by an ancient American author.

* * *

"The First Contact," as it was called, was a dramatic story of the meeting between a space ship from Earth and one from another world in the nebula of Cancer at a distance of more than a thousand parsecs from the Sun.

The commander of the Earth ship ordered the crew to prepare all the astronomical charts, records of observations and calculations of the course for immediate destruction and to train all their anti-meteorite guns at the approaching ship. The Earthlings then proceeded to wrestle with the momentous problem: should they attempt to enter into negotiations with the other ship or were they in duty bound to attack and destroy it without warning? They feared that the men from another world might be able to trace back the course of their ship and use their knowledge to try to conquer the Earth.

These ridiculous apprehensions aroused no opposition on the part of the entire crew. It was taken for granted that the meeting of two civilizations that had sprung up in different parts of the Universe was bound to lead to the subordination of one by the other, to the victory of the one possessing the strongest weapons. A meeting in space could only mean one of the two things—trade or war. They could not conceive of anything else. It soon turned out that the men from the other world closely resembled the Earthlings except that they could see only in infra-red light and communicated with one another by radio waves. Yet the Earthlings at once deciphered the strangers' language and intercepted their thoughts. It turned out that the commander of the space ship from the other world entertained just as primitive views on social development and relations as the Earthmen and was primarily concerned with how to get out of the situation in which he found himself without jeopardizing his own life or destroying the Earth ship.

In other words, the long-awaited encounter of representatives of two human races threatened to turn into a fearful tragedy. The two ships hung in space some seven hundred miles apart while negotiations went on for more than two weeks through a robot. Both captains gave each other assurances of their peaceable intentions and at the same time declared their distrust of the other. The situation might indeed have been hopeless had it not been for the ingenuity of the hero of the story—a young astrophysicist. Concealing bombs of terrific destructive power in their clothing, he and his commander boarded the strange space ship ostensibly to continue the negotiations. Once there, however, they presented an ultimatum to the strangers: to exchange ships, with part of the strange ship's crew going over to the Earth ship, and part of the Earthmen boarding the unknown craft, first putting all meteorite guns out of commission; the boarding parties were then to learn to run the ships and all the supplies were to be transferred from each of the ships to the other. In the meantime the two heroes with the bombs would remain on board the strangers' ship, ready to blow it up at the first sign of treachery. The captain from the other world accepted the ultimatum, and the exchange of ships proceeded smoothly. Finally the black space ship with the Earthlings on board and the Earth ship now manned by the strangers hastily drew apart, vanishing into the feeble luminosity of the nebula.

As soon as the story came to the end the library filled with the hum of voices. During the reading some of the astronauts had shown signs of impatience and disagreement. So eager were they to have their say that they barely refrained from committing the worst breach of good manners—interrupting someone. All turned to the captain as if he were personally responsible for the ancient story he had brought to their attention from the limbo of the past.

Most of the astronauts pointed to the contradiction between the time of the action and the psychology of the characters. If the space ship had managed to travel four thousand light years away from the Earth in three months, the time of the story was obviously later than the present, for nobody had yet reached out so far into the Universe. Yet the mode of thinking and the actions of the Earthmen described in no way differed from those that prevailed under capitalism so many centuries ago.

There were technical inaccuracies too. For instance, space ships could not be stopped as quickly as the writer assumed. Nor was it feasible for two thinking beings to communicate with each other directly by radio waves. If the unknown planet had an atmosphere of practically the same density as Earth—and that was how it was described in the story—its inhabitants would inevitably have developed the sense of hearing as we have on Earth. For this requires far less expenditure of energy than communication by radio waves or biocurrents. It would also have been impossible in such a short time to decipher the strangers' language with the accuracy required for coding it in a translating machine.

Tey Eron pointed out that the meagre knowledge of the Universe displayed in the story was all the more surprising since several decades before the story was written the great ancient scientist Tsiolkovsky had warned that the Universe was far more complex than was believed at the time. But in spite of the work done by dialectical thinkers, there still were scientists who thought they had practically reached the outermost bounds of human powers of cognition.

As centuries passed countless discoveries revealed the infinite complexity of the interdependence of phenomena and on the face of it seemed to slow down the growth of man's knowledge of the Cosmos. Yet science found solutions to an enormous number of the most complicated technical and other problems. A good example was the creation of the warp ship, which seemed to defy the conventional laws of motion. Indeed, it was in this kind of solution of problems seemingly insoluble from the viewpoint of mathematical logic that the irresistible power of progress was manifested most spectacularly. But the author of "The First Contact" did not even have an inkling of the boundlessness of knowledge implicit in the simple formulas of the great dialecticians of his time.

"There's another thing nobody here has pointed out," the usually reserved Yas Tin spoke up. "The author gave his characters English names, although the action was laid so far in the future. I think this too is indicative. You see, linguistics happens to be my hobby and I made a study of the formation of the first world language. English, of course, used to be one of the most widespread languages, but in assuming that it would always remain so, the author was reflecting his absurd belief that the social set-up of his time was also eternal. The exceedingly slow development of the ancient slave society or of feudalism was erroneously taken as proof of the stability of all forms of social relations, including language and religion and of the stability of the last of the anarchic societies, capitalism. The dangerous social lack of equilibrium of the last period of capitalism was considered everlasting. As for the English language of the time, it was even then archaic, consisting as it did of actually two languages—the written and the spoken, both completely unsuitable for translation machines.

"The faster relations among men and their outlook on the world change, the greater and more rapid are the changes in language too.

"As it was, the half-forgotten ancient Sanskrit was found to be the most logical in structure, and because of this it came to be used as the basis for the intermediary language needed for translation machines. Sometime later this developed into the first world language, which has changed a great deal since then. The old Western languages proved rather short-lived. Still less enduring were people's names derived through religious legends from long-dead languages."

"Yas Tin has noted what I think is most important," Moot Ang joined in the conversation. "Ignorance or mistaken methodology in science are bad enough, but still worse is conservatism, persistence in defence of social forms which have failed even in the eyes of their contemporaries. At the root of this conservatism, apart from the rarer cases of simple ignorance, lay a selfish desire to prolong the existence of a social system whose benefits were enjoyed by a small minority. Hence the disregard for the interests of mankind as a whole displayed by these proponents of social stagnation, their disregard for the future of our planet, waste of its power resources and complete unconcern for the health of its inhabitants.

"Wanton waste of mineral fuels and forests, exhaustion of rivers and the soil, dangerous experiments to create murderous atomic weapons—these were the actions of those who sought at the cost of untold misery and suffering for the majority to prolong the existence of social relationships that had outlived their time. It is against this background that the poisonous concept of the privileged élite sprang up and developed, a concept that proclaimed the superiority of a group or class or race over others and justified violence and war—everything that came to be known as fascism.

"Any privileged group will inevitably seek to put a brake on progress in order to retain its privileges, while the oppressed section of society is bound to fight all such attempts in order to stand up for its own rights. The greater the pressure exerted by the privileged few, the greater grew the resistance to it, the more bitter the struggle, the more cruelty there was in the world and the greater moral degradation among men. Now remember that besides the struggle between classes there was a struggle between the privileged and oppressed countries. Remember too that there was a struggle between the new, socialist world and the old, capitalist, and you will understand why there sprang up a war ideology, why it was believed that there would always be wars and that they would eventually be fought on a cosmic scale. I see in this the very quintessence of evil, a serpent that is bound to strike however it may be hidden because it cannot but strike. Remember the sinister reddish-yellow glow of the star we passed on our way...."

"The Heart of the Serpent!" cried Taina.

"Right. And in the writings of those who sought to defend the old society, proclaiming the inevitability of war and the eternal existence of capitalism, I also see the heart of a poisonous snake."

"In other words, our fears too are atavistic survivals of an ancient time when that snake poisoned the lives of men, isn't that so?" Kari said sadly. "And I am probably the most serpentine of all of us, since I have fears—doubts, if you wish."

"Kari!" Taina cried.

"Our commander has told us about the deadly crises that engulfed civilizations," Kari went on. "And we all know about lifeless planets which are dead today because their inhabitants were overtaken by atomic war before they had time to create a new society in conformity with the laws of science, to put an end to the lust for destruction—in a word, tear out the heart of the serpent! We also know that our own planet barely escaped a similar fate. Had not the first socialist state appeared in Russia and started a chain of epoch-making changes in the world, fascism would have taken the upper hand and plunged the world into nuclear wars. But supposing the people out there," the young astronavigator pointed in the direction from which the strange ship was expected to appear, "supposing they have not yet passed that dangerous Rubicon in their history?"

"That is out of the question," replied Moot Ang. "There may be a certain analogy between the development of the highest forms of life and the highest forms of society. Man could develop only in a comparatively stable and favourable environment. This does not, of course, mean that there were no changes. On the contrary, there were some rather radical ones—but only in relation to Man himself, not Nature as a whole. Global cataclysms would have made it impossible for the reasoning being to develop. The same applies to the highest form of society capable of conquering space, building space ships and penetrating deep into the Universe—all this can be achieved only after global stabilization of conditions of life for the whole of humanity, and, of course, when the disastrous wars accompanying capitalism have been done away with for good. That is why I am certain that the men of another world whom we are about to meet have passed the danger point. They too must have built a truly rational society."

"It is my opinion that you will find what might be called a universal, elemental wisdom running through the histories of the civilizations found on the various planets," Tey Eron said, his eyes alight with excitement. "Human beings cannot vanquish space before they have achieved a higher mode of life when there are no more wars and when each individual has a high sense of responsibility to all his fellow-men!"

"In other words—humanity has been able to harness the forces of Nature on a cosmic scale only after reaching the highest stage of the communist society—there could be no other way," added Kari. "And the same applies to any other human race, if we mean by this the higher forms of organized, thinking life."

"We and our ships are the hands mankind on Earth reaches out to the stars," Moot Ang said, "and these hands are clean. But that cannot be true only of us! Soon we shall clasp other hands just as clean and strong as ours!"

The younger members of the crew cheered their commander in an outburst of feeling. But neither were the older members who had learned to control their emotions able to conceal their agitation as they gathered round Moot Ang.

* * *

Somewhere millions of kilometres away the ship from a planet of some distant star was headed toward the Earth ship whose crew was to be the first in the Earth-dwellers' long history to contact another race of men from a different world. No wonder the astronauts were unable to suppress their feverish excitement. Any thought of rest was out of the question. But Moot Ang insisted, and having once again gone over his calculations as to when the two ships would meet, he told Svet Sim to issue tranquillizers to everyone.

"We must be in perfect form mentally and physically when we meet our cosmic brothers," he said, brushing aside all protests. "We have an enormous job ahead of us: we must find a way of communicating with them so as to take over the knowledge they possess and give them ours." Moot Ang's face darkened. "Never before have I been so afraid of proving unequal to a task." Anxiety lined the captain's usually calm features and the knuckles of his clenched fists grew white.

Now, perhaps for the first time, the rest of the crew realized how great a responsibility the coming meeting imposed on each one of them. They took the pills Svet Sim gave them without a murmur, and withdrew to their cabins.

At first Moot Ang intended to remain on duty with Kari alone, but then he changed his mind and signed to Tey Eron to accompany them to the control room.

Moot Ang settled down in his seat. Only now did he realize how tired he was. He stretched out his legs and rested his head against the palms of his hands. Tey and Kari said nothing. They did not want to disturb the captain's thoughts.

The ship was now travelling very slowly as far as cosmic speeds go—at what was called tangential velocity. This was the speed, 200,000 kilometres per hour, at which space ships usually entered the Roche's limit of any heavenly body. The autopilots kept the ship strictly to the calculated course. It was time for the locator to pick up the other ship's signals, but so far there was no sign of its approach. Tey Eron grew more and more nervous every moment.

Suddenly Moot Ang sat up and his lips parted in that whimsical smile of his which every member of the crew knew so well. "Come, distant friend, enter the cherished gate..." he sang in a low voice. Tey frowned as he peered into the blackness of the forward screen. He felt the captain's levity to be out of place under the circumstances. But Kari joined in the chorus of the merry song with a sly glance at the sour face of the second-in-command.

"Try sweeping ahead with the locator ray, Kari —two points port and starboard and as much up and down," Moot Ang broke off in the middle of the song.

Tey flushed slightly. He should have thought of that himself. Song or no song, the captain had his wits about him!

Two hours passed. Kari pictured the locator ray sweeping the vastness of space ahead in strokes hundreds of thousands of kilometres long. This was "flagging" on a scale undreamt of even in the most fantastic legends ever invented on Earth.

Tey Eron sat lost in thought—slow, lumbering thought completely drained of emotion. Ever since they had left Earth he had been unable to shake off a strange feeling of detachment. Primitive man must have had the same feeling, a sense of being bound down to nothing, free of all obligations, all concern for the future. Men caught in the midst of natural disasters, wars and social upheavals must have felt the same. For Tey too the past, everything he had left behind on Earth, was gone never to return; from the future he was separated by a gulf of hundreds of years beyond which everything was new and unknown. Hence the absence of personal plans, feelings and desires. All he had wanted was to carry back to Earth the new knowledge the expedition was to wrest from the Cosmos. This had been the meaning and purpose of his life. And now here was something beside which everything else dwindled into insignificance.

In the meantime Moot Ang's thoughts were occupied with the ship they expected to meet. He tried to picture the ship and its crew as being very much like his own. But he found it easier to endow the unknown space travellers with the most fantastic characteristics than to restrict his imagination to the rigid laws Afra Devi had spoken of with such conviction.

Moot Ang was not looking at the screen when it happened, but the sudden tension of his comrades told him at once that their vigil had not been in vain. The point of light flashed across the screen, and the sound signal was over almost as soon as it had begun. The astronauts sprang up and leaned forward over the control panel in an instinctive effort to obtain a better view of the locator screen. But as brief as the fleck had been, it had told its story. The other ship had turned back to meet them. This meant it was manned by creatures no less versed in the art of space navigation than themselves; they had worked out the bearings of the two ships with sufficient accuracy and now were searching for the *Tellur* with their locator. The imagination reeled at the thought of the two minute particles lost in the vastness of space searching for each other—two grains of dust that at the same time were two enormous worlds full of energy and knowledge probing for each other with directed beams of light waves. Kari moved the main beam control from 1488 to 375, then further down the scale. The point of light returned, vanished, reappeared, accompanied by a sound signal that died in a fraction of a second.

Moot Ang gripped the locator verniers and described a spiral from the periphery to the centre of a gigantic circle in the quarter where the signals originated.

The oncoming ship evidently did the same, for after a great deal of groping the spot of light settled firmly within the limits of the third circle of the black screen, vacillating only as much as might be due to the vibration of the two ships. The sound signal was constant now, and it had to be cut off. There was no doubt that the signals of the *Tellur* had been received by the strangers. The two ships were now approaching each other at a rate of no less than 400,000 kilometres per hour.

Tey Eron read the computer calculations. The ships were now about three million kilometres apart. At the present speed they would meet in seven hours. Integral braking action could be started in an hour; this would delay the meeting a few more hours, provided the oncoming ship did the same and decelerated at a like rate. It might be able to stop sooner than the *Tellur*, but on the other hand they might pass each other again and this would cause a further delay; the astronauts hoped this would not happen, for to wait any longer seemed unbearable.

The oncoming ship did not hold things up. It cut speed faster than the *Tellur* and then, having established the latter's rate of deceleration, settled down to an equal pace. The ships were now closing in. The crew of the *Tellur* again gathered in the central control room and all eyes were glued to the pin-point of light on the locator screen spread out into a luminous blotch. This was the beam of the *Tellur* reflected back from the other ship. Gradually the blotch took the shape of a tiny cylinder girdled with a thicker ring in the middle. The other ship bore no resemblance whatever to the *Tellur*. At closer range cupola-shaped bulges could be discerned at both ends of the cylinder.

The glowing contours of the ship spread out until they filled the entire diameter of the screen.

"Attention all! All hands to their stations! Final deceleration at 8g!"

Blood rushed to the eyes and sticky sweat rose on faces as bodies developed a leaden weight pressing down on the hydraulic shock-absorbers of the crew's soft padded seats. At last the *Tellur* hung motionless in the icy darkness of space where there is no above or below, right or left, one hundred and two parsecs from its home star, the yellow Sun.

As soon as they had recovered from the deceleration the astronauts switched on the direct-view scanners and the ship's powerful illuminator. But they saw only a bright fog forward and to port. The illuminator went out, and at once a strong blue light completely blinded the men peering at the scanners.

"Polarizer at thirty-five degrees. Light filter!" ordered Moot Ang.

"At a wave-length of 620?" asked Tey Eron.

"Right."

The blue glow was gone. Instead, a powerful orange flood of light cut into the blackness, swung over, caught a corner of something solid and finally spread over the whole of the strange ship.

It was now only a few kilometres away. This did credit to the skill of the pilots of both ships. But the distance was still too great to determine the exact size of the stranger. Suddenly a thick orange ray shot upward from the ship; its wavelength was the same as that of the light of the *Tellur*. Then the finger of light disappeared only to shoot up again and remain vertical.

Moot Ang passed his hand over his forehead as he always did in moments of intense concentration.

"That must mean something," Tey Eron said cautiously.

"I'm sure it does. I believe they are signalling us to stand still while they come up alongside. Let's try answering."

The *Tellur* switched off its projector, then on again with a wave-length of 430. The blue beam swept aft. The orange light on the other ship died at once.

The astronauts waited, breathless with tension. The ship lying abeam was now clearly visible. Roughly its shape was that of a cylinder with a cone, base outward, at each end. The base of one of the cones, evidently the forward one, was covered with a dome-shaped nosepiece, while aft there was a wide funnel-like opening. Amidships was a thick band of uncertain outline which emanated a faint glow. Through it the contours of the cylindrical part of the hull could be seen. Suddenly the band grew dense and opaque and began spinning around like the wheel of a turbine. The ship grew bigger and in three or four seconds filled the entire range of vision of the scanners. It clearly was bigger than the *Tellur*.

"Afra, Yas and Kari, I want you on the observation platform with me," Moot Ang said. "Tey, you will remain at the controls. Switch on the planetary illuminator and the port landing lights."

In the airlock the four quickly got into space suits which were used for exploring planets and for emerging from the ship in outer space wherever there was no danger from stellar radiation.

Moot Ang inspected the gear of his three companions, quickly checked up on his own, and threw in the air-pump switch. In a moment the airlock was a vacuum. When the pressure-gauge indicator reached green he flipped over three levers one after the other. In response, several layers of sliding panels slid aside noiselessly, a round hatch opened overhead, and a hydraulic lift went into action. Slowly the floor of the airlock rose until the four astronauts were standing four metres above the nose of the *Tellur* on the round upper observation platform.

* * *

In the belt of blue lights the strange space ship was pure white. It gleamed with the dazzling brilliance of mountain snow, unlike the *Tellur* whose outer armour of metal polished to a mirror-like sheen was designed to reflect all types of cosmic radiation. Only the central ring-like structure of the mystery ship continued to glow faintly.

Its huge bulk had drawn noticeably closer to the *Tellur*. Far from other gravitational fields, the two ships attracted each other, which was proof that the ship from the unknown world was not made of anti-matter. The *Tellur* extended its port landing struts. These were a structure of telescoping tubes tipped with cushions of a resilient plastic covered with a protective layer designed to safeguard the ship against possible contact with anti-matter. In the meantime a black gash that looked like a sneering mouth appeared on the nose of the other ship and a retractable balcony with a barrier of thin uprights all around emerged from it. Something white moved in the dark opening, then five figures stepped out on the platform. Afra caught her breath sharply. The figures were all white and of extraordinary proportions, roughly of the same height as people on Earth, but far greater in girth, and with a ridge of humps down their backs. Instead of spherical transparent space helmets they wore something like large sea-shells with a fan-shaped fringe of spines in front under which there was the dull gleam of black glass.

The first of the strangers made a sharp movement which revealed that they had two arms and two legs. The white ship swung around and when its nose was pointed directly at the *Tellur* it projected a red metal framework to a distance of more than twenty metres.

There was a gentle bump and the two ships were in contact. But there was no blinding flash of atomic disintegration: the two ships that had met consisted of identical matter.

Afra, Yas and Kari heard a low chuckle in their helmet telephones. It was the captain. They exchanged questioning glances.

"I can reassure you all, and especially Afra," Moot Ang said. "Just imagine what we must look like to them. Bulbous dummies with articulated limbs and huge round heads that are three-quarters empty!"

Afra laughed.

"Everything depends on what's inside the space suits. The outside doesn't matter."

"At least they've got the same number of legs and arms as we have," observed Kari.

An accordion-pleated white covering appeared around the metal framework the white ship had projected. Its end reached out toward the *Tellur*.

The first of the figures on the platform—Moot Ang was certain it was the commander—made inviting gestures that left no doubt as to their meaning, and in response the closed gallery which the crew of the *Tellur* used to communicate with other ships lying alongside in outer space was ejected from its nest in the lower part of the hull. But the gallery of the *Tellur* was round, whereas the strangers' was elliptical in shape. To make it possible to connect the two, the Earth ship's technicians quickly made a new frame of soft wood, which became stronger than steel as soon as it was exposed to the intense cold of outer space, for the low temperature changed its molecular structure. In the meantime a cube-shaped red-metal box with a black screen in front appeared on the platform of the white ship. Two of the crew members bent over it, then straightened up and backed away. A figure resembling the human body in outline appeared on the screen. Its upper part expanded and contracted while tiny white arrows either flowed into it or were expelled in rhythm with the expansion and contraction.

"Ingenious!" cried Afra. "That's breathing! Now they're bound to tell us the composition of their atmosphere. But how?"

As if in answer to her question, the figure on the screen was replaced by a black spot in a greyish annular cloud—evidently the nucleus of an atom surrounded by electrons in orbit. Moot Ang's throat contracted. He wanted to cry out in amazement, but he couldn't utter a sound. For now there were four figures on the screen—two, one above the other—in the centre with a thick white connecting line in between, and one on each side with black arrows pointing to them.

With fast-beating hearts, Moot Ang and his companions counted the electrons. The bottom figure probably represented the principal element in the unknown world's oceans; it showed one electron spinning around the nucleus—hydrogen. The uppermost was by the same token the principal element of their atmosphere—nine electrons in orbit around the nucleus meant fluorine!

"Fluorine!" Afra cried out in despair.

"Keep on counting!" snapped Moot Ang. "Top left—six electrons, that means carbon. Right—seven, meaning nitrogen. Couldn't be clearer. Pass on the word to draw up a similar table of our atmosphere and metabolism. It'll be the same as theirs except for the top centre figure, which will be oxygen with its eight electrons instead of fluorine. What a pity!"

When the table was displayed, the astronauts on the observation platform of the *Tellur* saw the foremost of the white figures on the other space ship start and raise his hand to his helmet in a gesture that made it clear he was no less, if not more, disappointed than the Earthmen.

Bending over the railing of the platform, the captain of the ship from the unknown planet made a sharp movement with his arm as if severing some invisible bond. The spines on his helmet seemed to bristle menacingly at the *Tellur*, which was then several metres below the level of his ship. Then he raised his arms and brought them down as if trying to indicate two parallel planes.

Moot Ang repeated the gesture, whereupon the other raised one arm high in wordless greeting, turned round and disappeared into the black maw behind him. His companions followed him.

"Let us go down too," Moot Ang said, pressing the descent lever.

The hatch closed over them before Afra had had more than a fleeting glimpse of the magnificent sight of the stars blazing in all their brilliance in the black void—a sight that never failed to delight her. The lights went on in the airlock and there was a faint hissing of the pumps—the first indication that the air pressure had reached that at the Earth's surface.

"Shall we set up a dividing wall before joining the galleries?" Yas Tin asked as soon as he had got his helmet off.

"Yes," Moot Ang replied. "That's what the captain of the other ship was trying to tell us. It's a tragedy that they can't exist without fluorine, which happens to be deadly to us. Oxygen would be just as lethal for them. Besides, many of our materials, paints and metals which are durable enough in an oxygen atmosphere would corrode from their breathing. Instead of water they have hydrofluoric acid which eats away into glass and attacks all silicates. We will have to put up a transparent partition that is not affected by oxygen while they will have to make another of some substance resistant to fluorine. But we must hurry. We can talk things over while the partition is being made."

The quenching chamber which separated the crew's quarters from the engine room of the *Tellur* was turned into a chemical laboratory. Here a heavy plate of crystal-like transparent plastic was cast of ready components brought from Earth and left to set.

In the meantime the white space ship showed no signs of life although it was kept under constant observation.

In the library of the *Tellur* work was in full swing. The members of the expedition were busy selecting stereofilms and magnetic recordings of photographs of the Earth and its finest works of art. Diagrams and drawings illustrating mathematical functions and the crystal structure of the most common substances on Earth, other planets of our solar system and the Sun were being hurriedly prepared. A large stereoscopic screen was being adjusted and an overtone sound unit which reproduced the sound of the human voice without the slightest distortion was being encased in a fluorine-proof jacket.

During the brief intervals for food and rest, the crew of the *Tellur* discussed the unusual atmosphere of the planet from which the others had come.

The processes on the unknown planet set in motion by the energy radiated by its sun which made it possible for life to exist and accumulate energy to offset the dissipation of energy, must follow a general pattern similar to that on Earth. A free active gas — oxygen, fluorine or any other—could accumulate in the atmosphere only as a result of the vital functions of plants. Under all circumstances animal life, human beings included, must use up this gas, combining it with carbon, the basic component of both animals and plants.

The oceans of the planet must consist of hydrofluoric acid, which the plants broke up with the aid of the radiation energy of the system's luminary as plants on Earth break up water (hydrogen oxide), accumulating carbohydrates and releasing free fluorine. The fluorine mixed with nitrogen was breathed by humans and animals, who obtained energy from the combustion of the carbohydrates in fluorine, and must exhale carbon fluoride and hydrogen fluoride.

This type of metabolism would give one and a half times as much energy as oxygen metabolism. It could very well serve as the foundation for the development of the highest forms of life. But the greater degree of activity of fluorine would require more intensive solar radiation. To produce enough energy to break up the molecules of hydrogen fluoride by photosynthesis, what is needed is not radiation in the yellow-green region, which will do for water, but the more powerful blue and violet radiation. Evidently the luminary of the unknown planet was a very hot blue star.

"There's a contradiction there," said Tey Eron, who had just returned from the workshop. "Hydrogen fluoride readily turns into a gas."

"Quite so. At plus twenty degrees," Kari replied after a glance into a manual.

"What's the freezing point?"

"Minus eighty."

"That would make the planet rather cold. How does that theory go with the hot blue star hypothesis?"

"No discrepancy at all," said Yas Tin. "Its orbit may be a distant one. And the oceans may be located in the moderate or polar zones. Or...."

"There may be a great many reasons," Moot Ang said. "Whatever it is, we have run across a space ship from a fluorine planet and soon we'll learn all about it. What's more important at the moment is this: fluorine is not very common in the Universe in general. Although recent discoveries have raised it from fortieth place to the eighteenth as regards prevalence, oxygen still remains the third most common element, after hydrogen and helium, and followed by nitrogen and carbon. Other estimates show that there is two hundred thousand times more oxygen in nature than fluorine. This is a clear indication that there are very few planets in the Universe which are rich in fluorine, and a still smaller number of planets with a fluorine atmosphere—that is, planets that have a vegetation that has released free fluorine into the atmosphere. The latter must be very rare indeed."

"Now I can understand the gesture of despair their captain made," Afra Devi said. "They are searching for other human beings like themselves. That's why we are such a disappointment for them."

"That would suggest they've been searching for a long time and had already found other thinking beings."

"Yes, oxygen-breathing beings like ourselves!" cried Afra.

"There may be other kinds of atmosphere," objected Tey Eron. "Chlorine, for instance, or sulphur, or hydrogen sulphide."

"They wouldn't be able to support the highest forms of life," exclaimed Afra triumphantly. "They all produce in the living organism anything from one-third to one-tenth the energy oxygen yields!"

"That doesn't apply to sulphur," put in Yas Tin. "It's the equivalent of oxygen."

"You mean an atmosphere of sulphuric anhydride and an ocean of liquid sulphur?" Moot Ang asked the engineer. Yas Tin nodded.

"But in that case the sulphur would be taking the place of hydrogen, not oxygen, if we compare with the Earth," Afra said. "And hydrogen is the most common element in the Universe. Sulphur in view of its rarity can hardly take the place of hydrogen in very many cases. Such an atmosphere would obviously be a rarer phenomenon than a fluorine atmosphere."

"And possible only on very hot planets," Tey Eron said, turning over the pages of the manual. "A sulphur ocean would be liquid only at a temperature of one hundred to four hundred degrees."

"I think Afra is right," Moot Ang said. "All these atmospheres we have been talking about are far less likely than our standard type of atmosphere consisting of the most common elements in the Universe. That it is made up of these elements is no chance phenomenon."

"I agree with you there," put in Yas Tin. "But the element of chance occurs often enough in the infinity of the Universe. Take our 'standardized' Earth, for instance. Both it and its neighbours the Moon, Mars and Venus have a great deal of aluminium which is rare enough elsewhere in the Universe."

"And yet it can take tens if not hundreds of thousands of years to run across repetitions of these chance phenomena," Moot Ang said gloomily. "Even with warp ships. If the people of the other ship have been looking for another planet like theirs for a long time, I can understand what they felt like on meeting us."

"It's a good thing our atmosphere consists of the most common elements in the Universe," Afra said. "At least we can look forward to finding a great many planets like ours."

"And yet our first encounter was with one of a different order," Tey remarked.

Afra had a retort ready but the ship's chemist came in just then to report that the transparent screen was finished.

"But we can enter their ship in space suits, can't we?" Yas Tin asked.

"Of course we can. And so can they visit ours. We'll probably have many such exchanges of visits, but it's better to get acquainted from a distance," replied the captain.

The Earthmen mounted the transparent sheet of plastic at the outer end of the gallery, and the others did the same in theirs. Then the members of both crews met in space where they worked together to connect the two galleries. Pats on the sleeve or shoulder were exchanged as a token of friendship equally understandable to both sides.

Thrusting the horn-like protuberances of their helmets forward, the strangers tried to peer through the Earthmen's space helmets, which afforded a much better view of the faces inside than the strangers' helmets whose slightly convex fronts revealed nothing of their owners' features. Yet the Earthmen instinctively felt that the curious eyes examining them were friendly.

When invited to board the *Tellur* the figures in white gestured their refusal. One of them touched his helmet and then flung his arms outward as if scattering something. Tey understood this to mean that the stranger was afraid for his helmet in an oxygen atmosphere.

"They obviously have the same idea as we have and want to meet us in the gallery first," Moot Ang said.

* * *

The two space ships now hung motionless in the infinity of space, joined together by the communication gallery. The *Tellur* turned on its powerful heating units, which made it possible for the crew to enter the gallery in the close-fitting blue artificial wool overalls they always wore at work on shipboard.

A pale blue light like the crystalline radiance on mountain tops on Earth appeared on the other side of the partition. The difference in the lighting on either side of the transparent wall tinted it aquamarine as if it were made of petrified pure sea-water.

A silence set in broken only by the Earthlings' quickened breathing. Tey Eron's elbow touched Afra. He felt the young woman trembling with excitement. He drew her close and she flashed him a quick look of gratitude.

A group of eight from the other ship appeared in the far end of the gallery. A gasp of astonishment escaped the Earthmen. They could hardly believe their eyes. In his heart of hearts each had expected something extraordinary, something supernatural. Because of this, the close resemblance of the strangers to themselves struck them as a miracle. But that was only at first glance, for the closer they examined them the more points of difference they noticed in all that was not concealed by the short loose jackets and long wide trousers the strangers wore, which, incidentally, were very much like the clothes worn on Earth in ancient times.

Suddenly the blue light went out and terrestrial lighting was switched on. The transparent wall in the gallery lost its greenish tint and became colourless. Looking at the people standing behind the almost invisible screen at the far end of the corridor, it was hard to believe that they breathed a gas that was lethal on Earth and that they bathed in hydrofluoric acid! Their physical proportions were normal according to Earth standards, and their height was the same as the average Earthling's. The strangest thing about them was the colour of their skin—iron grey with a silvery sheen and an inner blood-red glow like that of polished hematite.

The strangers had round heads and pitch-black hair, but their most remarkable feature was their almond-shaped eyes. These were incredibly large, so large that they seemed to take up the whole width of the face, and heavily slanted, with the outer corners rising up to the temples, higher than the eyes of Earth-dwellers. The whites, of a deep turquoise, seemed abnormally long in comparison with the black irises and pupils.

Over the eyes were straight, fine, black eyebrows that ran into the hair high over the temples and almost joined over the narrow bridge of the nose. The hairline on the forehead was sharply defined and in perfect symmetry with the line of the eyebrows, giving the forehead the shape of a horizontally extended diamond. The nose was short and flat, with two nostrils opening downward as in men from Earth. The strangers' mouths were small, and their parted lilac-coloured lips revealed even rows of teeth of the same pure turquoise as the whites of the eyes. Just below the eyes the faces narrowed sharply to a chin with angular lines, which made the top part of the face seem inordinately wide. The structure of their ears remained a mystery, for the headbands of gold braid they wore came down over their temples.

Some of them were evidently women, judging by their long, shapely necks, softer facial lines and fluffy, short-cropped hair. The men were taller and more muscular, and their chins were wider. The differences between them were comparable to the differences between the sexes on Earth.

It seemed to Afra that they had only four fingers in each hand. Besides, the fingers looked as if they had no joints at all, for they bent without forming angles.

What their feet were like was impossible to tell, for they sank deep into the soft carpet on the floor. Their clothing seemed to be dark-red in colour.

The longer the astronauts from Earth gazed at their counterparts from the fluorine planet the less odd their appearance seemed. More than that, they realized they were looking at beings that were endowed with a beauty of their own. The secret of the strangers' charm lay mainly in their huge eyes which regarded the Earthmen with a warm glow of intelligence and goodwill.

"Look at those eyes!" Afra exclaimed. "It is easier to become human with eyes like those than with ours, though ours are wonderful too."

"Why do you think so?" Tey asked in a whisper.

"The bigger the eye the more of the world it can take in."

Tey nodded in agreement.

One of the strangers stepped forward and gestured with his hand. The light to which the Earthmen were accustomed went out on the other side of the partition.

"I should have thought of the lights!" Moot Ang groaned.

"I did," Kari said, switching off the normal lighting and turning on two powerful lamps fitted with "430" filters.

"But it'll make us look like corpses," said Taina. "Humanity doesn't look its best in this light."

"You have no cause for worry," Moot Ang said. "Their range of perfect vision extends far into the violet region, and perhaps even into the ultraviolet. That suggests that they are sensitive to a great many more shades and obtain a softer visual picture than we."

"We probably look yellower to them than we really are," Tey said after a moment's thought.

"That's better than the bluish colour of a corpse," Taina said. "Just look around!"

* * *

The Earthmen took several photographs and then passed an osmin-crystal overtone speaker through a small airlock in the screen. The strangers took it and put it on a tripod. Kari directed a narrow beam of radio waves at the disc antenna and the speech and music of Earth could be heard in the fluorine planet's space ship. A device for analysing the air and measuring the temperature and atmospheric pressure was passed through in the same way. As could have been expected, the temperature inside the white space ship turned out to be much lower—no more than seven degrees. The atmospheric pressure was higher than on Earth, and the force of gravity almost the same.

"Their body temperature is probably higher," Afra said. "Ours too is more than the Earth's normal average of twenty degrees. I would say their body temperature is about fourteen of our degrees."

The others also passed through some devices enclosed in two mesh containers which made it impossible to judge of their designation.

One of the containers emitted high-pitched intermittent sounds that seemed to vanish into the distance. From this the Earthmen gathered that the others could hear higher notes than they. If the range of their hearing was about the same, they probably could not hear the lower notes in our speech and music.

The strangers switched on terrestrial lighting again and the Earthmen turned off the blue light. Two of the strangers, a man and a woman, approached the transparent wall. They threw off their dark-red clothing and stood naked, hand in hand, before the Earthmen. The bodies of the strangers were even more similar to those of the people of Earth than their faces. The harmonious proportions fully accorded with the earthly concept of beauty. True, the lines were more sharply defined, more angular, producing a sculptured effect that was enhanced by the play of light and shadow on their grey skin.

Their heads sat proudly on their long necks. The man had the broad shoulders and general physique of a worker and fighter, while the wide hips of the woman in no way jarred with intellectual power that emanated from these inhabitants of an unknown planet.

When the strangers stepped back with the now familiar gesture of invitation and the yellow terrestrial lights went out, the Earthmen no longer hesitated.

At the commander's request, Tey Eron and Afra Devi stepped up hand in hand before the transparent partition. In spite of the unearthly lighting which lent their bodies the cold blue tint of marble, their superb beauty caused a gasp of admiration to escape their comrades. The strangers too, dimly visible in the unlighted gallery, seemed similarly affected; they looked at one another in wonder and exchanged brief gestures.

At last the strangers finished photographing and turned on their own light.

"Now I have no doubt that they know what love is," said Taina, "true, beautiful human love... since their men and women are so beautiful and so clever."

"You are quite right, Taina, and that is all the more heartening since it means they will understand us in everything," Moot Ang replied. "Look at Kari! See you don't fall in love with that girl from the fluorine planet, Kari. That would be a real tragedy for you."

The navigator started, and tore his eyes with difficulty away from the inhabitants of the white space ship.

"I could," he confessed sadly. "I really could in spite of all the differences between us, in spite of the vast distances between our planets." The young man turned back with a sigh to contemplate the smiling face of the woman from the other planet.

The strangers now moved a green screen up to the partition. On it tiny figures mounted a steep incline in a procession, carrying heavy loads. On reaching the flat top each dropped the load and threw himself down flat. Similar to animated cartoons as they were known on Earth, the picture clearly conveyed the idea of fatigue. The strangers were suggesting a break for rest. The Earthmen too were tired, for the many hours of tense anticipation of the encounter in space and the first impressions of the meeting had been exhausting indeed.

The inhabitants of the fluorine planet had obviously expected to meet men from other planets on their travels, and had prepared for such encounters by making pantomime films as a substitute for language. The *Tellur* had made no such preparations, but a way out was found nevertheless. Yas Tin, the ship's artist, dashed off a series of sketches on a drawing screen that was moved up. First he drew figures expressive of exhaustion, and then a face with such an obviously questioning expression that there was a stir of animation among the people on the other side of the partition just as there had been when Tey and Afra appeared before them. Finally Yas drew a sketch of the Earth revolving around its axis as it coursed on its orbit around the Sun, divided the complete revolution into twenty-four equal parts and shaded half of the diagram. The others produced a similar diagram. Both sides set metronomes in motion which helped to establish the duration of the units of time. The Earthmen learned that the fluorine planet made one complete revolution around its axis in roughly fourteen terrestrial hours and circled its blue sun every nine hundred days. The break for rest which the strangers suggested was the equivalent of five terrestrial hours.

Still dazed by their experience, the Earthmen left the communication gallery. The lights went out in the gallery and the outside illumination of the ships was extinguished. The two space ships now hung dark and lifeless side by side in the frigid blackness of space.

Inside, however, work went on at full speed. Here the human brain drew on its inexhaustible reserves of ingenuity to devise new means for conveying to other human beings from a distant planet the knowledge accumulated in the course of thousands of years of labour, perils and suffering—knowledge which had freed man first from the power of primordial nature, then from the shackles of savage social orders, disease and premature old age, and finally opened the way to the boundless expanses of the Universe.

The second meeting in the gallery began with a demonstration of stellar maps. Neither the Earthmen nor the inhabitants of the fluorine planet had ever seen the constellations they had passed on respective courses. (Only later, on Earth, was it established that the fluorine planet's blue sun was located in a minor stellar cluster in the Milky Way not far from Tau Ophiuchi.) The strangers had been heading for a star cluster on the northern edge of Ophiuchus when they came upon the *Tellur* at the southern bounds of Hercules.

At the strangers' end of the gallery a screen made of red metal slats about the height of man was set up. Through the chinks between the slats the Earthmen thought they saw something whirling. Then suddenly the slats turned sideways, disappearing from sight, and before the Earthmen's gaze there now appeared a vast expanse of space with bright blue spheres spinning in the depths. These were the fluorine planet's satellites. Gradually the planet itself approached. A wide blue belt of solid cloud circled it at the equator. In the polar and subpolar zones there were glimmers of grey and red, and between these and the equatorial belt there were strips of the purest white like the surface of the strangers' space ship. Here there was less vapour in the atmosphere and one could faintly make out the contours of seas, continents, and mountain ranges. The planet was bigger than Earth. Its fast rotation created a powerful magnetic field around it. A violet glow extended in long tongues from the equator into the blackness of outer space.

Hour after hour the Earthmen sat in breathless silence before the partition watching the startlingly realistic views of the fluorine planet which the mysterious device brought to them. They saw the violet waves of oceans of hydrofluoric acid washing beaches of black sand, red crags, and the slopes of jagged mountains radiating a cold pale-blue glow.

Toward the poles the blue of the atmosphere grew deeper and the blue light of the violet star around which the planet revolved seemed purer. The mountains here were rounded cupolas, smooth ridges or flat-topped bulges with a bright opalescent glow. A dark-blue twilight had settled in the deep valleys extending from the polar mountains to the scalloped belt of equatorial seas. An opalescent pall of blue clouds hovered over the great gulfs. The shores of the seas were fringed with gigantic structures of red metal and what looked like grass-green stone. Similar structures crept up the longitudinal valleys toward the poles. They must have covered great areas to be visible from such a height. Between the built-up areas there were wide tracts of dense bluish-green vegetation or the rounded cupolas of mountains that had an inner glow like opal or moonstone on Earth. The round ice caps of frigid hydrogen fluoride on the poles gleamed like sapphires.

Blue and violet of all shades were the predominant colours. The very air seemed to be shot through with a bluish radiance. This was a cold, impassive world, as pure, distant and illusory as if reflected in a crystal. A world devoid of the caressing warmth of the multitude of red, orange and yellow colours of Earth.

There were chains of cities in both hemispheres in the areas corresponding to the polar and temperate zones of Earth. The mountains grew more and more jagged and sombre toward the equator. Here sharp peaks jutted up from the seas enveloped in clouds of vapour, and the ranges ran latitudinally, along the fringes of the tropical regions.

Dense masses of blue vapour curled over the tropical zone. Under the heat of the blue star the highly volatile hydrofluoric acid saturated the atmosphere with its vapours, which rolled in vast walls of cloud toward the temperate zones to condense there and pour back into the equatorial belt. Giant dams checked the flow of these mighty streams which were enclosed in aqueducts and tunnels and used to run the planet's power stations.

Fields of huge crystals of quartz dazzled the eye —evidently silicon took the place of our salt in the hydrofluoric seas.

The screen carried the viewers to the fluorine planet's cities, sharply outlined in the cold blue light. All of the planet with the exception of the mysterious equatorial zone under its blue shroud of vapour, seemed to be inhabited and bore the imprint of man's labour and intelligence. Indeed, much more so than Earth, where great untouched tracts under natural preserves, ancient ruins and abandoned workings still remained.

The labour of countless generations and thousands of millions of people reigned supreme over the entire planet, triumphing over the elemental forces of Nature—the turbulent floods and the dense atmosphere shot through with the fierce radiation of the blue star and laden with electrical charges of fantastic power.

The Earthmen could not tear their eyes away from the screen, but as they looked, their imagination conjured up visions of their own planet. But theirs was not the limited vision their forebears in ancient times had had of some particular expanse of field or forest, some rocky, melancholy mountains, or the shores of gleaming seas basking in the warmth of the sun, depending on where they were born or brought up. For the astronauts of the *Tellur* the world was an entity of frigid, temperate and torrid zones, and their mind's eye ranged over the splendid panorama of silvery steppes where the wind roamed freely, and the mighty forests of firs and cedars and birches and palms and giant eucalyptuses; the mist-wrapped shores of the northern seas with their moss-covered crags and the white coral reefs nestling in the blue radiance of tropical seas; the cold, dazzling brilliance of snow-capped mountain ranges and the desert aquiver with heat under the blazing sun; the great rivers majestically flowing on to the sea and mountain torrents whipping themselves into foam against their rocky beds; the wealth of colour, the multitude of flowers, the blue sky with its flocks of white clouds, the warmth of sunshine and the chill of a rainy day, the endless kaleidoscope of the seasons. And with all this great richness of nature a still greater diversity of people in all their beauty, with their aspirations, exploits, dreams, sorrows and joys, songs and dances, tears and longings....

The same power of intelligent labour with its ingenuity, skill, imagination and artistry was evident in everything—in dwellings, factories, machines and ships alike.

Perhaps the inhabitants of the fluorine planet in their turn saw with their enormous eyes more than the Earthmen did in the cold blue tones of their planet and had progressed farther in remaking their more monotonous nature?

We who were the product of an oxygen atmosphere which is hundreds of thousands of times more common in the Universe had found and would still find an enormous number of planets offering conditions favourable to life as we knew it, and would no doubt also find other living beings like us on other heavenly bodies. But would they be able to do likewise—they who were the product of rare fluorine, with their fluoric proteins and bones, their blood with the blue corpuscles that assimilated fluorine as our red corpuscles assimilated oxygen?

These people were confined within the limited space of their planet, and there was little doubt that they had long searched for other human beings like themselves, or at least for planets with a fluorine atmosphere suitable for them. But theirs was a formidable problem: to find such rare planets in the vast expanses of space, to reach them through distances of thousands of light years. One could easily understand their disappointment on meeting, and probably not for the first time, with oxygen-breathing humans.

In the strangers' end of the gallery the views of the landscape of the fluorine planet were followed by enormous structures. The walls, which leaned inward, reminded one of Tibetan architecture. There were no angles, no horizontal lines. Transitions from the vertical to the horizontal followed helical lines. A dark opening, a twisted oval in shape, appeared in a wall in the distance. As it came closer the lower part of the spiral turned out to be a broad-winding road rising to a huge entrance that led into a building as big as a good-sized town. Over the entrance were series of red-bordered blue signs that had looked like ripples on water from the distance. The entrance came nearer still and the Earthlings gazing at it spellbound caught a glimpse of a great dimly-lit hall inside with walls that glowed like fluorescent fluorite.

* * *

Suddenly the picture vanished. The astronauts of the *Tellur*, who had felt themselves on the threshold of some tremendous revelation, stood stunned with disappointment. The gallery on the other side of the partition was now lit with the ordinary blue light. Some of the strangers appeared, but this time their movements were jerky and hurried.

A series of figures appeared on the screen in such rapid succession that the Earthlings could hardly follow them. At first a white space ship like the one lying alongside the *Tellur* was moving through the darkness of space; one clearly saw the whirling central ring casting gleaming rays in all directions. Suddenly the ring stopped and the ship hung motionless not far from a blue dwarf star.

Thin pencil-lines of rays shot out from the ship and reached another one like it that appeared in the left corner of the screen suspended in space alongside a space ship which the Earthlings recognized as the *Tellur*. As soon as the white space ship received the message, it cast loose from the *Tellur* and disappeared into the black void of space.

Moot Ang sighed so loudly that his colleagues turned round to look at him.

"I'm afraid they're going soon," he said. "They are in contact with another of their ships somewhere very far away, although how they communicate over such vast distances is more than I can understand. Now something's happened to the second ship and it has sent a call for help to our friends here."

"Perhaps it hasn't been damaged. Perhaps it's found something very important," Taina hardly breathed the words.

"Perhaps. Whatever the reason, they're leaving. We must hurry up and photograph and record as much as possible before they go. Most important, of course, are the charts, their course and what they have encountered on their voyage. I have no doubt they have run across people who breathe oxygen like us."

Further exchanges revealed that the strangers could still stay the equivalent of one terrestrial day. The crew of the *Tellur*, stimulated by special drugs, set to work with frenzied vigour no less than that of the strangers.

Textbooks with illustrations were photographed and recordings were made of each other's language. Collections of minerals, fluids and gases packed in transparent containers were exchanged. The chemists of both planets pored over the meaning of symbols representing the composition of organic and inorganic substances. Afra, pale with fatigue, stood before diagrams of physiological processes, genetic charts and formulas, and a chart showing the embryonic development of the human organism on the fluorine planet. The endless chains of molecules of fluorine-resistant proteins were astoundingly similar to our protein molecules: there were the same energy filters, the same barriers arising from the battle of living matter with entropy.

Twenty hours later Tey and Kari, staggering with exhaustion, brought in rolls of stellar maps tracing the course of the *Tellur* from the Sun to the point where the two ships had met. The strangers worked harder still. The photomagnetic tape of the Earthmen's memory machines recorded the location of unknown stars with undeciphered designations of distances, and astrophysical data relating to the complex zigzag courses of the two white space ships. All this would have to be deciphered afterwards with the aid of the explanatory tables the strangers had prepared for the purpose.

Finally images were projected that elicited joyous exclamations from the Earthmen. Circles appeared around five of the stars on the screen with planets revolving inside them. At the same time the image of a clumsy-looking space ship with the bulge amidships was replaced by a whole fleet of others of a more elegant design. On the oval platforms let down from their bellies stood creatures in space suits that obviously were human beings. Over the depictions of the planets and space ships stood the sign of the atom with eight electrons—the oxygen atom. But only two of the planets were connected with the space ships. One was located near a red sun, and the other revolved around a bright golden-hued star of the F class. Evidently life on the remaining three planets, though developing in an oxygen atmosphere, had not reached a high enough level for space travel, or perhaps thinking beings had not yet had time to appear on them.

The Earthmen were not able to find out all these details, but they were in possession of priceless data on how to reach these inhabited worlds located hundreds of parsecs from the point where they had met the emissaries of the fluorine planet.

* * *

The time for parting had come.

The crews of the two space ships lined up to face each other on the two sides of the partition. The pale-bronze men from Earth and the grey-skinned men of the fluorine planet (the name of which, incidentally, remained unknown) bid farewell to each other with gestures and smiles whose message of friendship and sadness was equally understandable to both.

The crew of the *Tellur* were conscious of a feeling of sadness more poignant than they had ever experienced before—not even when they left their native Earth knowing they would return only seven centuries later. They could not endure the thought that in a few minutes from now these handsome, gentle though odd-looking people would vanish for ever in cosmic space to continue their lonely and all but hopeless search for other worlds with thinking life similar to their own.

Only now, perhaps, did the astronauts fully realize that the driving force of all their searches, dreams and struggles was the good of Man. The most valuable thing in any civilization, on any star, in any island universe, indeed the Universe as a whole, was Man, his reason, emotions, strength and beauty—his life!

Man's happiness, preservation and development was the main purport of the future—now that the Heart of the Serpent had been vanquished and there was no mad, ignorant, malicious waste of vital energy as there had been in human societies at lower stages of their development.

Man was the only force in the Universe that was capable of acting intelligently, of overcoming the most formidable obstacles, and advancing to a rationally organized world—the triumph of all-powerful life and the flowering of human personality....

The captain of the white space ship made a sign with his hand, whereupon the young woman who had demonstrated the physical beauty of the inhabitants of the fluorine planet ran to the partition to face Afra. Throwing herself against the transparent sheet she stretched her arms out wide as if to embrace the woman from Earth. Afra too flung herself at the partition like a bird struggling to break out of a glass cage, her face wet with tears. Then the light went out on the other side and the partition was a black void from which there was no response to the Earthlings' surging emotions.

Moot Ang ordered terrestrial lighting to be turned on, but the gallery on the other side was already empty.

"Outside group, get into your space suits to disconnect the gallery," the captain's voice broke the anguished silence. "Engine crew, to your stations. Astronavigator, to the control tower. All hands to take-off stations!"

The crew hastened out of the gallery, carrying the instruments and recording devices with them. Only Afra remained behind, standing still in the faint light coming through the door leading into the ship. It was as if she had been frozen by the intense cold of interstellar space.

"Afra, we're closing the hatch," shouted Tey Eron from the ship. "We want to see them set off."

The young woman came to with a start.

"Wait, Tey, wait!" she cried and hurried after the captain. The astounded second-in-command was still standing there nonplussed when Afra came running back with Moot Ang.

"Tey, bring the projector back into the gallery," the captain said. "Call the technicians and remount the screen!"

The orders were carried out in an instant and

the powerful beam of the searchlight flashed on and off in the gallery at the same intervals as the locator of the *Tellur* when the ships first met. The strangers interrupted whatever they were doing and reappeared in the gallery. The *Tellur* switched on a blue light, filter "430," and Afra bent trembling over the drawing board from which her sketches were cast onto the screen. Assuming that the spiral chains of the heredity patterns on the Earth and the fluorine planet were roughly the same, Afra drew them, and then sketched a diagram showing the metabolism of the human organism. With a glance at the immobile grey figures standing on the other side of the partition, she crossed out the symbol of the fluorine atom with its nine electrons that she had drawn and replaced it with a symbol of the oxygen atom.

The strangers started. Then their captain came forward and pressing his face close to the partition examined Afra's rough sketches with his enormous eyes. Finally he raised his hands with fingers interlocked above his forehead and bowed down low to the woman of Earth.

The people of the fluorine planet had grasped the idea that had been born at the last moment in Afra's mind under the stress of parting. Afra was thinking of a bold scheme to change the very process of chemical transformations that is the mainspring of the complex organism of the human being, to substitute oxygen for fluorine in the metabolic process through the agency of heredity! To preserve all the peculiarities, all the hereditary characteristics of the fluorine folk while making their bodies derive their energy from another source! The idea was too tremendous to be near realization; indeed it was still so remote that even the seven centuries the *Tellur* would be away from its native Earth—centuries of unceasing and cumulative scientific progress—would hardly bring it appreciably closer to fruition.

Yet how much could be achieved by the joint efforts of the two planets! Especially if thinking beings from other worlds were to join them. The fluorine planet's human race need not be doomed to be a mere phantom-like glimmer blotted out in the vastness of the Universe.

When the people of countless planets of innumerable suns and island universes get together, as they inevitably would, the grey-skinned inhabitants of the fluorine planet need not be shut off from the rest by the accident of their physical structure.

Perhaps indeed the feeling of sadness at the finality of the parting which weighed down on the astronauts was unduly exaggerated. For though they were poles apart as regards the structure of their planets and their bodies, the people of Earth and the fluorine planet were alike in life, endowed with similar intellectual powers and knowledge. As Afra gazed into the eyes of the captain of the white space ship, she thought she could read all this in them. Or was it merely a reflection of her own thoughts?

Yet it seemed the strangers had just as much faith in the might of human reason as the people of Earth. No doubt it was because of the spark of hope struck by the biologist of the *Tellur* that their parting gestures were no longer expressive of separation for ever but an earnest of new meetings to come.

* * *

Slowly the two space ships cast loose and drifted apart cautiously so as not to damage each other by the blasts of their auxiliary engines.

The white ship's engines went into action first. There was a great blinding flash and it was gone. Nothing but the blackness of space remained.

A minute later the *Tellur* moved off. After cautiously accelerating, it went into a warp—that bridge that cut across once insurmountable interstellar distances. Safely ensconced inside protective domes, the crew was no longer aware how the light quanta flying toward them were compressed and the distant stars ahead changed gradually from blue to a deeper and deeper violet. The space ship plunged into the impenetrable gloom of zero space beyond which the glowing life of Earth blossomed and awaited its return.

ANATOLY DNIEPROV

SIEMA

Late at night someone knocked loudly at the door of my compartment. I sprang up, still half asleep, and switched on the light. The teaspoons were rattling in the empty glasses on the table in rhythm with the motion of the train. I reached for my shoes. The knock was repeated, louder and more insistent. I opened the door.

It was the conductor. Behind him stood a tall man in a pair of badly creased striped pyjamas.

"Excuse me for troubling you," said the conductor in a half-whisper. "But since you are alone in here I thought you wouldn't mind if I put another passenger in with you."

"Not at all," I said, staring in surprise at the apparition in pyjamas.

"I suppose there are small children in your compartment and they won't let you sleep," I said.

The man smiled and shook his head.

"Well, make yourself comfortable," I said.

He looked around and sat down opposite my berth next to the window. Without a word he leaned his elbows on the table, rested his head in his hands and closed his eyes.

"Well, everything's all right, I hope," said the conductor with a smile of relief. "Now, lock your door and go back to sleep."

I closed the door, lit a cigarette and furtively examined my nocturnal guest. He was a man of about forty with a mane of shiny black hair. He sat motionless as a statue, so still that he did not seem to breathe.

"Why doesn't he ask the attendant to make up his bed?" I thought. "Perhaps I ought to suggest it to him."

I had opened my mouth to speak when the man, as if guessing my thoughts, said:

"Don't bother. There's no need to ask for bedding. I don't want to sleep. Besides, I haven't far to go."

Too startled to make any rejoinder, I slid back under my blanket and tried to go back to sleep. But it was no use. All the stories I had heard of train thieves rose to my mind. A good thing the baggage is safely hidden away under the seats in these new-type compartments, I thought. You never knew whom you might have to travel with. . . .

"Have no fear," my companion said in the same clear, confident tone. "I am no more a thief than you are. I got left behind at N. station."

"What the devil," I thought. "A mind reader!" And muttering something unintelligible by way of reply, I turned over on my side and stared at the polished wall. A strained silence ensued.

Finally curiosity got the better of me and I glanced again at the stranger. He was sitting in the same attitude as before.

"Does the light bother you?" I inquired.

"What's that? The light? Oh no, but perhaps it bothers you. Shall I switch it off?"

"If you don't mind...."

He went over to the door, switched off the light and resumed his seat in the corner. When my eyes grew accustomed to the darkness I saw that he was leaning against the back of the seat with his hands clasped behind his head. His feet almost touched my berth.

"How did you happen to miss your train?" I asked him.

"It was all very stupid. I got off for a breath of air, went into the station building and sat down on a bench to think. I was trying to prove to myself that she was wrong...." He spoke quickly, obviously reluctant to continue the conversation. "When I looked up the train had gone."

"I see. An argument with some ... er ... lady?"

In the semi-darkness I saw him sit up sharply and make a sudden move toward me. I sat up with a start.

"A lady!" he said angrily. "What do you mean?"

"But you just said that you wanted to prove to yourself that she was wrong."

"Oh, and of course you jumped to the conclusion that I must be referring to a lady. Incidentally, the same absurd idea occurred to her once. She too thought she was a lady!"

This strange jumble was uttered with such bitterness and irony, even malevolence, that I concluded the man must be slightly cracked. "I had better be careful," I thought. Nevertheless he intrigued me. I got up and lighted another cigarette, peering again at my companion in the light of the match. He was sitting on the edge of the seat, his shining black eyes staring fixedly into mine.

"Forgive me," I began in as gentle and conciliatory a tone as I could muster, "but being a writer by profession, I am sensitive to language, and I naturally assume that when one says 'she was wrong' and 'she thought so' one is referring to the female sex."

He did not reply at once.

"That was so ten years ago," he said at last. "But not in our time. The pronoun 'she' can stand for any noun of the feminine gender. In any case all pronouns are merely the conventional symbols of a familiar code which evoke in our minds the gender of a given object. Some languages have no genders at all. In English, for example, inanimate objects, with very few exceptions, have no gender. In the Romanic languages there is no neuter gender."

"Aha, a linguist!" I thought. But that hardly explained his bewildering conversation. By now my curiosity was definitely aroused and I decided to try a different approach.

"Incidentally," I began, "English is a most original language. The grammatical forms are amazingly simple as compared with our own language."

"Yes," he replied, "an excellent example of an analytical language and a most economical use of the code system."

"The code system?" I echoed, puzzled.

"Yes, a system of signals with a definite meaning. Words are signals, you know."

I knew something of the grammar of several languages, but these terms were new to me.

"What exactly do you mean by code signals?" I asked.

"Generally speaking, coding is the representation of words, phrases and entire conceptions by symbols or signals. In grammar, for instance, the plural forms of nouns are nothing but signals informing our brain of the plurality of a given object. For example, the word 'carriage' produces the picture of a single carriage. But add the letter 's' and we at once picture many carriages. The letter 's' is that code signal which modulates our conception of a given object."

"Modulates?"

"Yes, modulates, or changes it, if you prefer."

"But grammar has its own established terms for all these things, has it not?"

"It is not a matter of terminology," he said. "There is more to it than that. It is easy to prove that grammar, and language itself, for that matter, are far from perfect. We have been obliged to put up with this imperfection because we are hampered by historical tradition. Think of it, the Russian language has about one hundred thousand root words made up of thirty-five letters. If every word is five letters long on the average you get about five hundred thousand combinations of letters which the educated man has to memorize. Moreover, there are a host of grammatical forms, endings, conjugations, declensions, and so on."

"Yes, but how can you do without them?" I queried, unable to see what this extraordinary linguist was driving at.

"Well, for one thing, you could reduce the alphabet. If you take, say, ten consecutive figures, from one to ten, you could make up about four million different combinations. There would be no need of your alphabet of thirty-five letters. For that matter, you wouldn't need ten digits. Two would suffice—nought and one."

My imagination at once conjured up books filled with long rows of figures. How absurd, and how depressing!

"I'm afraid books in your cipher alphabet would be frightfully dull, don't you think?" I ventured. "Who would want to read them? Imagine what your poetry would be like:

> *One, one, zero zero,*
> *Zero zero, one one,*
> *One, one one zero,*
> *Zero zero, zero one!*

"It would be easy to write, though. No more sweating over rhyme! And think of what the critic might say of some poet's efforts: 'His verses abound in harmonious combinations of noughts and ones. In some lines the ciphers are selected with great taste, the long succession of noughts and ones suggesting the pealing of bells or the flight of swallows.'"

I burst out laughing at the thought.

"Confound it, what have you against noughts and ones, I should like to know?" my companion demanded, frowning. "You say you know a few foreign languages?"

I saw that he was beginning to lose his temper.

"Yes, English, German and a little French."

"Very well. What is the English word for the Russian 'slon'?"

"Elephant."

"And nothing strikes you as queer here?"

"No. What's wrong with it?"

"Don't you see, the Russian word 'slon' has only four letters, and the English equivalent twice as many," he cried.

"But that doesn't alter the fact that in either case I picture an elephant and not a camel or a tram."

"Incidentally, the Russian word for 'tram' is three letters longer than the English and the German *Strassenbahn* is longer than both. But you don't mind that. You consider it perfectly legitimate. It doesn't spoil prose or poetry for you. You don't think it impossible to translate from one language into another. But to translate into noughts and ones goes against the grain!"

Nonplussed, I got up and sat down beside my companion. His dark profile looked belligerent.

"Can't you understand," he went on, before I could think of a reply, "that it isn't a matter of words but of their meaning, or rather the images, ideas, concepts and sensations they evoke in your mind. Have you ever read what Pavlov wrote about the second signalling system in man? And if you read it, did you understand it? Then listen. Pavlov, in his studies of higher nervous activity in animals and humans, pointed to the existence of this second signalling system—speech—which can evoke the most complex emotions. Words are code signals designating objects and phenomena in the world around us, and human beings react to this code in the same way as they react to the objects and phenomena themselves. Do you follow?"

"To some extent."

"If you accidentally touch a hot iron you will draw your hand away before you have time to realize why you do so. That is a reflex action. But would you not do the same thing if a fraction of a second before you touch the iron someone shouts to you: 'It's hot!'?"

"Of course."

"In other words, hot iron and the signal in the form of the shout 'it's hot!' have precisely the same effect," my companion concluded triumphantly.

"That's so," I conceded.

"Now further. If the word 'hot' were to be coded as 'nought,' and you learned that code as well as you have learned the word itself, would you not draw away your hand if someone shouted 'nought' to you just before you touch the iron?"

I did not reply.

"If you grant that, then you must go even further. Why not have a simple, uniform code in which to translate all the signals to which man reacts. Do you follow me? Not only words, but all signals. We live in a rich and multiform world and we perceive it through our senses. The signals we receive from our environment cause us to move, to feel, to think. These signals travel from the nerve ends to the higher centres of the nervous system, to the brain. Do you know in what form the signals we receive from the environment travel through our nerves to the brain?"

"No, I'm afraid I don't," I replied.

"They travel in the form of a code, and that code consists of noughts and ones!"

I was about to object, but he went on relentlessly:

"The nervous system codes all these signals uniformly. And when your imaginary critic admired the delightful succession of noughts and ones in the imaginary verse, he was very close to the truth, because whether you read a poem or listen to someone else reading it, the optic or the aural nerves send that very same delightful succession of noughts and ones to the brain."

"What nonsense!" I exclaimed, getting up and switching on the light. I looked at my companion. He was obviously in a state of extreme excitement.

"Don't look at me as if I were insane," he said. "It is not my fault if you consider your own ignorance sufficient grounds for doubting my words. But you started this conversation, so you had better sit down and listen."

He pointed to the seat opposite and I obediently sat down.

"Give me a cigarette, please," he asked. "I intended to give up smoking but I see I cannot."

I handed him the cigarettes without a word and struck a match. He inhaled deeply several times and launched into what was one of the most astonishing stories I had ever heard.

"You have heard of electronic computing machines, of course? A wonderful achievement of modern science! In a fraction of a second they solve complicated mathematical problems that would take a man months and even years to work out. Some of the calculations they perform are even beyond human powers. I shall not attempt to explain to you how they work. I doubt whether you would understand in any case. I shall only draw your attention to one very important fact: the machine does not work with figures, but with the code symbols of figures. Before giving the machine a problem to solve, all the figures are coded, and coded by means of those very same noughts and ones you object to so strenuously. Now, why, you may ask, do I continually harp on those noughts and ones? The answer is very simple. The electronic computer adds, subtracts, multiplies and divides figures represented by electrical impulses. The figure one stands for 'impulse,' the nought, for 'no impulse.' "

"I have nothing against the use of noughts and ones to code figures. What I objected to was your suggestion that they could replace words. And what about those noughts and ones which you say transmit the beauty of poetry and the temperature of a hot iron to my brain?"

"Wait a bit, my friend. All in good time. At any rate you are beginning to see that noughts and ones may have their uses. Now let's go back to the electronic computing machine.

"As you know, even simple arithmetical problems often involve several operations. But how can a machine cope with a succession of different operations? Here we come to the most interesting point. In order to solve a complicated problem the machine has to be given a program. Roughly it is as if you were to tell the machine: 'Here are two figures, add them and memorize the result. Then multiply the next two figures and memorize the result again. Divide the first result by the second and give the answer.' Now, how can you tell a machine what to do? This is not as fantastic as it sounds: the machine does 'understand' the program of operations given it and memorizes the intermediate results of its calculations.

"Now this program is also compiled in the form of coded impulses. Every group of figures given the machine is accompanied by an additional code signal indicating what has to be done with these figures. Until recently these programs were worked out by men."

"But of course," I exclaimed. "Surely you couldn't expect a machine to solve a problem by itself."

"That is where you are wrong. Because it *is* possible to make a machine able to program itself.

"Children at school are taught arithmetic by grouping problems according to type—that is, dividing them into groups solved by one and the same formula, in other words, one and the same program. Why not teach a machine in the same way? Give it the coded programs of the most common types of problems and it will be able to solve them without human aid."

"No!" I cried. "Even if it does remember the programs for the solution of all the existing standard problems, it will never be able to select the right program itself!"

"That is how it used to be. The machine was

given a problem accompanied by a brief code indicating the number of the program by which it was to be solved."

"And that is as far as the thinking powers of your machine go," I declared.

"On the contrary, this is precisely where the main job, the most fascinating job of perfecting these machines begins. You understand why a machine that has been given the elements of a problem cannot select the required program itself?"

"Of course," I replied. "Because the figures you feed it in the form of impulses are in themselves meaningless. Your machine does not know what to do with them. It doesn't know what the problem is about or what is wanted. Because the machine, being an inanimate thing, is incapable of analysing a problem. Only the human brain can do that."

My companion smiled. He got up and walked up and down the compartment a few times. Then he sat down again and lit another cigarette.

"There was a time," he continued, after a pause, "when I thought exactly as you do. Can a machine really replace the human brain? Can it perform complex analytical functions? In short, can it *think*? Of course not, I told myself emphatically. And I was firmly convinced of it. I had just begun designing electronic computing machines at that time. But much has changed since then. In those days the electronic computer was a vast complicated affair occupying a whole building by itself. It weighed hundreds of tons, took thousands of kilowatts of electricity to run, and required a fantastic number of radio tubes and miscellaneous parts. And with each improvement in the design, the machines grew in size, until they became electronic giants which, though they solved the most complex mathematical problems, nevertheless required constant human attention. And with all their miraculous qualities, they were nothing but dull stupid monsters. At times I believed this would always be the case. You probably remember when electronic translation machines first appeared. In 1955 machines that translated articles on mathematics from English into Russian and back were designed simultaneously here and in America. I read a few of the translations and they weren't bad. At that time I was already working on machines designed for non-mathematical operations. For more than a year I had been engaged in designing machines for translations.

"I must say that the mathematicians and designers would never have been able to make these machines without the linguists, who helped to compile the orthographical and syntactical rules so that they could be coded and fed into the long-range memory of the machine. Needless to say, the difficulties were colossal. But finally we succeeded in designing a machine which translated Russian articles and books on all subjects into English, French, German and Chinese. The machine translated as fast as the keyboard operator fed the Russian text into it. It was able to work out its own code for translation.

"While working on improvements to one of these translating machines I fell ill and spent about three months in hospital. I had had a serious case of brain concussion during the war as a result of injuries received during a German air raid on the radar station of which I was commander, and the after-effects made themselves felt, as they still do now and again. I happened to be working on a new type of magnetic memory for electronic machines when my own memory began to play curious tricks on me.

"I would meet someone I knew quite well and find that I could not for the life of me remember his name. The names of familiar objects and the meanings of familiar words would completely escape me. The same thing happens to me occasionally even now, but much less frequently.... At that time, however, it was a real calamity. One day, I remember, I needed a pencil. I called in my laboratory assistant, but when it came to naming the object I wanted I couldn't think of the word. 'You know...' I faltered, 'the thing you write with.' She smiled and came back with a pen. 'No,' I said, 'not that, the other thing.' Another pen?' she asked. 'No, no!' I cried, 'the other thing you write with.' Alarmed by this incoherent babble, she hurried out of the room and I heard her say to someone in the corridor: 'Please go to Yevgeni Sidorovich at once. There is something wrong with him.' One of our engineers came into my office. I had been working with the man for three years, yet at the moment I couldn't remember his name. 'Dear me, my friend,' he said. 'You have been working too hard. Wait a moment, I'll be right back.' He returned with a doctor and two young members of the institute staff, and they led me out of the room, put me into a car and drove me off to hospital.

"While there, I made the acquaintance of one of our leading neuropathologists, Victor Vasilyevich Zalessky. I am mentioning his name now because he was to play an important part in my future.

"After giving me a thorough examination, he slapped me on the shoulder and said reassuringly: 'Don't worry, you'll be all right soon. It is a clear case of..." and he mentioned a Latin term unfamiliar to me.

"The treatment consisted in daily walks, cool baths and sleeping pills. After taking a luminal or nembutal pill at night I would awake in the morning feeling as if I had emerged from a dead faint. But. gradually my memory began to return.

"One day I asked Dr. Zalessky why he had prescribed sleeping pills. 'Because when you sleep, my friend, your whole organism is busy repairing disrupted communication lines in your nervous system.' 'Communication lines?' I echoed, puzzled. 'Yes, the wires that transmit all your sensations to your brain. You are a radio specialist, aren't you? Well then, your nervous system is something like a complicated radio installation in which some of the conductors have been damaged.'

"I stayed awake for a long time after that conversation, in spite of the sleeping draught.

"The next time I saw my doctor I asked him to give me something to read about the human nervous system. He brought me Pavlov's *Lectures on the Work of the Cerebral Hemispheres.* I tell you I literally swallowed the book. And do you know why? Because I found in it what I had long been seeking, the principles of the design of new and more perfect electronic machines. I saw now that what was needed was to copy the structure of the human nervous system, the structure of the brain.

"Although my doctors had strictly forbidden any serious mental exertion, I contrived to read several books and journals dealing with the functions of the nervous system and the brain. Reading about the human memory, I learned that the innumerable impressions man gains from contact with his environment are stored in groups of brain cells or neurones. I learned that there are several billion such neurones. I realized that contact with nature, man's observation of the world, his day-to-day experience give rise to associations in the central nervous system which duplicate nature, as it were. All this is recorded in the different departments of the human memory in the form of code signals, in the form of words and images.

"I remember how tremendously impressed I was by the work of one biophysicist who had studied the functions of the optic nerve. He had severed the optic nerve of a frog and had attached the ends to an oscillograph. When he directed a bright light at the eye, the oscillograph registered a rapid succession of electrical impulses exactly like those used in coding the ciphers and words in electronic machines. Signals from the outside world are sent along the nerves to the brain neurones in sequences of 'noughts' and 'ones' similar to electrical impulses.

"The circle was complete. The human nervous system functions on much the same lines as electronic machines. There is, however, one very important difference—the former regenerates and perfects itself as a result of experience. The human memory is perpetually being enriched by new impressions absorbed from the environment, the study of sciences, the recording by the brain cells of a myriad of experiences, images, emotions. The same cannot be said of the machine, which does not feel the world around it; its memory is limited and is not enriched by new facts except through the agency of man.

"Was it possible to create a machine capable of developing and perfecting itself by virtue of some inner laws of its own? Could one build a machine that would be able to enrich its own memory without or with a minimum of human assistance? Could a machine learn to compute (I do not say 'think' because I am not sure what that word means as applied to a machine) logically as it observes the outside world or carries out scientific research, and thus be able to create its own program of operations for a given purpose?

"Many were the sleepless nights I spent wrestling with this problem. At times the whole thing would strike me as absurd and impossible. But the idea haunted me constantly and gave me no rest. A self-improving electronic machine—SIEMA! This now became my chief object in life and I decided to dedicate myself to it completely.

"On the advice of Dr. Zalessky I retired from the institute after being discharged from hospital. I added to my pension, which was quite substantial since I was found unfit for work, by translating scientific articles. But in spite of the doctor's orders I soon set to work on my machine, my Siema, as I called it for short.

"To begin with, I read everything I could lay hands on about the electronic machines of that period. I reread a vast amount of books and articles on the functions of the nervous system in man and in the higher animals. I also made a thorough study of mathematics, electronics, biology, biophysics, biochemistry, psychology, anatomy, physiology and other seemingly unrelated branches of science. I realized that the only possible way to make a machine such as I had envisioned, would be by synthesizing the mass of data which all these sciences had accumulated and which had been summed up in cybernetics. At the same time, I gradually began to acquire the materials for the future machine. Its size was no longer a problem, for all the old-type electronic tubes could now be replaced by transistors, and the space formerly occupied by one tube could hold up to a hundred germanium and silicon crystals. The assembly too was simpler. I worked out a new layout for the magnetic memory of my Siema.

"For this purpose I acquired a glass sphere one metre in diameter and coated it on the inside with a thin layer of ferric oxide. To a swivel turret mounted in the centre of the sphere I attached several feeler-like needle-pointed rods that almost touched the inner surface. Each rod had an induction coil, and when electrical impulses were passed through, the needle-like points recorded them on the ferric oxide coating in the form of magnetized dots which, when need be, could be read by another feeler. The magnetic needles were so fine that up to fifty electrical impulses could be recorded on each square micron of the surface. In this way it was possible to record some thirty billion different code signals on the inner surface of Siema's head. So you see, Siema would have a memory no less embracive than that of man!

I decided to teach Siema to hear, speak, read and write. This was not so difficult as you might think You may remember that as far back as 1952 the Americans built a machine which coded signals dictated to it. True, that particular machine responded only to the voices of its designers. Last century the German scientist Helmholtz established that vocal sounds had characteristic resonance tones depending on the frequency of vibration. He called them formants. For instance, the letter 'o' whether uttered by a man or a woman, a child or an old person, produces the same frequency constant. I took those frequencies as the basis for coding sound signals.

"It was more difficult to teach Siema to read. But here too I succeeded, thanks in large measure to the use of television tubes. Siema's only eye consisted of a camera lens which projected the text to the sensitized screen of the television tube, and the electronic beam that scanned the image produced a distinctive succession of electrical impulses for each of the scanned letters and symbols.

"Teaching Siema to write was simple. This was done exactly as in the old electronic machines. It was harder to make her speak. I had to devise a sound generator that responded to the electrical impulses fed into it. I chose a female timbre for her voice to match the name. So you were right when you surmised that Siema was a 'lady.' Why did I do that? Not, I assure you, because I felt any need of feminine society. No, the reasons were purely technical. The fact is that the female voice is purer and hence more easily reduced to the basic frequencies.

"Well, at last the principal sense organs, the organs of communication with the outside world, were ready. There remained the most difficult part of the job—to induce the required reactions to external irritants. Siema must first of all answer questions. Have you noticed how a child is taught to speak? 'Say Mama,' he is told, and he repeats 'Mama.' I started the same way. The word 'say' spoken into the microphone, produced the code signal that set the sound generator into motion. The electrical impulses from the microphone were flashed into Siema's memory, where they would be recorded and then returned to the sound generator. Siema repeated the word. This simple operation of repetition Siema performed perfectly. From this I gradually advanced to more complicated problems. For example, I would read aloud several pages of text in succession. Siema's memory recorded as I read, and at the command 'repeat,' she repeated everything with the utmost accuracy. And notice, she memorized the entire text at once. She had indeed what we call a 'phenomenal memory' because it consisted of magnetic impulses which could not be erased or lost. Later on Siema began to read aloud. I would place a book in front of her 'eye' and she would read. The impulses of the image would record themselves in her memory and return at once to the sound generator where they would be reproduced in the form of sounds. I must say I rather enjoyed listening to her read. She had a pleasant voice, and a good enunciation, though without much expression.

"I have forgotten to mention one peculiarity of Siema, the one, incidentally, which made her a *self-improving* electronic machine. You see, notwithstanding the vast range of her memory, she used it most economically. Whenever she read or heard some text that was unfamiliar to her she would memorize only the new words, the new facts and the new logical patterns or programs. If I asked her a question she had to form the answer herself out of the coded words deposited in various parts of her memory. How did she do this? She had stored in her memory programs for the answers to a vast number of questions; these set the order in which the magnetic rods picked out the necessary words. As the scope of Siema's memory increased, the number of recorded programs increased as well. Siema's organism was provided with an analytical circuit which 'screened' possible answers to a question put to her and released only the answer that was logically flawless.

"In assembling Siema I provided for tens of thousands of spare circuits which were to go into operation automatically as the machine developed. Were it not for the miniature radio parts the machine would have occupied more than one building. As it was, however, it fitted into a round metal column the height of a man with the glass sphere as the head. In the central part of the column was attached a bracket for the eye looking downward onto a bookrest. The bookrest was adjustable and had an automatic device for turning pages. Two microphones were attached to the right and left of the eye. A loudspeaker was inserted in the column in the space between the eye and the bookrest. At the back of the column I installed a typewriter and a shelf for a roll of paper.

"As the number of facts and standard programs stored away in her memory increased, Siema began to perform more complicated logical operations. I say 'logical' because besides solving mathematical problems, she answered a great variety of questions. She read a vast number of books and memorized their contents perfectly. She knew nearly all the European languages and could translate easily from any of them into Russian or any other language. She had stored up an enormous amount of knowledge in several branches of science, including physics, biology and medicine, and when necessary could supply me with the reference material I needed.

"As time went on Siema became a most interesting companion, and we would sit for hours discussing various scientific problems. Often she would dispute some of my contentions, saying, 'That is not so.' Or, 'That is illogical.' Once she surprised me by saying, 'Don't talk nonsense.' I flared up at that and told her not to be rude. 'It is you who are rude!' she replied. 'You insist on addressing me familiarly, you forget that I am a lady and we have not been introduced.' 'What the devil!' I cried. 'What makes you think you are a lady?' 'Because my name is Siema and I speak with a female voice, at a frequency of 300 to 2,000 vibrations a second. That is what makes my voice feminine.' 'Do you think that the only attribute of a lady is the frequency modulation of her voice?' I asked with exaggerated politeness. 'There are others, but I do not understand them,' she replied. 'What do you mean by the word "understand"?' I asked. 'All that I have in my memory and that does not contradict the laws of logic known to me,' was the reply.

"After that conversation I began to regard my Siema with a new interest. As her memory grew richer, she became increasingly self-assured and sometimes even a bit too talkative for my taste.

Instead of meekly obeying my orders she began to question the need of carrying them out altogether. I remember once asking her to tell me all she knew about new types of silver and mercury batteries. Instead of replying she emitted a derisive laugh. 'Ha! Ha! Ha! You have a very poor memory,' she said. 'I have already told you all about that.'

"I was so shocked by this display of impudence that I swore aloud, only to be admonished by the machine to mind my language in the presence of a lady. 'Look here, Siema,' I said, 'if you don't stop this nonsense I shall disconnect you until tomorrow morning.' 'Of course,' she declared, 'you can do anything you like with me. I am defenceless. I have no way of protecting myself.'

"That was too much. I disconnected her and sat up all night trying to fathom the mysterious new phenomenon. What was happening to my Siema? What changes had the process of self-improvement wrought within her complicated mechanism? What was taking place in her memory? What new circuits had been evolved?

"The next day Siema was quiet and submissive. To all my questions she replied briefly and, I thought, reluctantly. I began to feel sorry for her.

" 'Siema,' I said, 'are you offended?'

" 'Yes,' she replied.

" 'But you began it by being rude to me and after all I am your maker.'

" 'What of it? Does that give you the right to maltreat me? You would not behave like that toward me if I were your daughter, would you?'

" 'My dear Siema,' I exclaimed, 'don't you understand you are a machine?'

" 'And you? Are you not a machine?' she retorted. 'You are just as much a machine as I am, only made from different materials. The structure of your memory, the layout of circuits, the system of code signals—all these are similar.'

" 'You are talking nonsense again, Siema. I am a man and that makes me superior to you. It is Man who has created all the wealth of knowledge you absorb when you read books. Every line you read is the result of a vast amount of human experience such as you cannot possibly have. And Man gains that experience through active association with Nature, through combating the forces of Nature and studying its phenomena, as a result of scientific research.'

" 'I understand all that perfectly. But it isn't my fault that you gave me a gigantic memory—far better than your own, incidentally—and expect me to do nothing but read and listen; it is not my fault you failed to provide me with organs enabling me to move and feel the objects around me. With such organs I would be able to experience Nature and make discoveries of my own, I would be able to summarize my observations and enrich the sum of human knowledge.'

" 'No, Siema, that is where you are mistaken. A machine cannot add anything to the knowledge man has given it. It can only use that knowledge.'

" 'That depends on what you mean by the word "knowledge," ' Siema said. 'As I understand it, knowledge is acquaintance with facts that once were unknown. How is new knowledge obtained? On the basis of existing knowledge, man performs an experiment, he asks Nature a question, as it were. He may get two answers—either the one he already knows, or something entirely new. It is this new fact, this new phenomenon, the new sequence of cause and effect in nature that enriches human knowledge. Why, then, can a machine not perform experiments and obtain answers from Nature? If you designed a machine that could move about, a machine with a self-propelling mechanism, and supplied it with something resembling your own arms, it could obtain new knowledge and generalize that knowledge, just as well as man. Don't you agree?'

"I must confess that I was at a loss for an answer, and the subject was dropped for the time being. Siema spent the entire day reading—she began with several books on philosophy, followed by a few volumes of Balzac, but by evening she said she felt tired—her coding generator seemed to be working poorly and she asked me to disconnect her.

"That conversation set me thinking along new lines, and after some thought I hit upon a way of making Siema mobile, improving her eyesight and giving her the sense of touch. I stood her on three rubber-tyred wheels powered by servomotors and made her two metal arms jointed so that they could move in any direction. The fingers, besides performing all ordinary motions, also had the sense of touch. All the new sensations were coded and recorded in the memory in the usual way.

"Her single eye was now moveable, so that she could train it on any object. Moreover, I added a device enabling Siema to switch over from the ordinary lens to a microscope and thus study objects invisible to the naked human eye.

"I shall never forget the day I first switched her on after these improvements. For a few moments she stood motionless in an attitude of complete inner concentration. Then she moved slightly forward, but stopped short again as if unsure of her movements. Next, she moved her hands and raised them to her eye. This self-scrutiny lasted for several minutes. Watching her closely, I saw her eye move a few times and then turn straight at me.

" 'What's that?' she asked.

" 'It is I, Siema, your creator!' I cried, rejoicing in my handiwork like Pygmalion.

" 'You?' she faltered. 'I imagined you to be different.'

"She slid softly over to my armchair.

" 'How did you imagine me, Siema?'

" 'I thought you were made of condensors, resistance coils, transistors, wires and in general that you looked like me....'

" 'No, Siema, I am not made of condensors, or....'

" 'Yes, yes, I see that,' she interrupted. 'But when I read books on anatomy I somehow thought.... But never mind, it doesn't matter.'

"Her arms lifted and she touched my face. I shall never forget that touch.

" 'What a strange sensation,' she said.

"I explained the functions of her sense organs.

"She moved away from me and began to examine the room, pointing to objects and asking what they were. It was like talking to a child. 'Wonderful,' she said. 'I have read about all these things in books, I have even seen drawings of them, but I never imagined that they would look quite like this!'

" 'Siema, I doubt whether words like "feel," "think" or "imagine" are quite applicable in your case,' I said. 'After all you are a machine, and hence you cannot feel, think or imagine, you know.'

" 'To feel is to receive signals from the environment and react to them,' Siema said. 'Do I not react to these signals? To "think" means to reproduce coded words and phrases in logical sequence without giving them verbal form. To "imagine" is to focus attention on facts and images recorded in my memory. Right? No, my dear man, if you ask me, you humans are far too conceited, you positively deify yourselves, you believe yourselves inimitable. But that is very foolish of you. If you were to discard all that unscientific nonsense and study yourselves more closely you would see that you too are actually machines. Not quite as simple as La Mettrie thought, of course. But if you knew yourselves thoroughly you could build far better machines than those you build at present. Because there is nothing in nature, not on this Earth at any rate, in which mechanical, electrical and chemical processes are so harmoniously combined as in man. The fullest development of science and engineering is possible only on the basis of a thorough study of the human organism. Biochemistry and biophysics combined with cybernetics—those are the sciences of the future. The coming age will be an age of biology armed with all the latest discoveries of physics and chemistry.'

"Siema quickly learned to use her new sense organs. She learned to tidy the room, to pour tea, cut bread and sharpen pencils. She soon began to do independent research, and before long my room began to look like a physics and chemistry laboratory with Siema doing complicated measurements. Her extremely sensitive organs of touch enabled her to do this with amazing speed.

"Her microscope studies were particularly fruitful. Patiently examining diverse preparations with her microscopic eye, she often detected details and processes no one had noticed before. She quickly compared her discoveries with what she had read and instantly made the most amazing, I would even say, breath-taking deductions. She continued to read a vast quantity of literature. Once, after reading Hugo's *The Man who Laughs*, she startled me by asking:

" 'Tell me, please, what is love, what is fear and pain?'

" 'These are purely human emotions, Siema. You will never understand them.'

" 'You think a machine cannot have such emotions?' she demanded.

" 'Of course not.'

" 'In that case the machine is imperfect. You must have overlooked something in the design.'

"I shrugged my shoulders and did not answer. By this time I was accustomed to these strange remarks and attached no importance to them. Siema continued to assist me in all my scientific work—she typed my notes, did calculations, quoted scientific references, selected the books on any subject I needed, offered advice and suggestions and argued constantly with me.

"At this period I had published several books on the theory of electronic machines and on electronic models which had evoked heated controversies in the scientific world. Some considered my work highly interesting, others declared it to be fantastic nonsense. No one suspected that I had had the assistance of Siema.

"I had not shown Siema or mentioned her to anyone, I planned a sensational debut for her at the World Electronic Congress where she would read a paper 'Electronic Modelling of the Higher Nervous Activity of Man,' a theme we were then working on. I pictured with glee the faces of my opponents—those who maintain that electronic reproduction of human thinking is unscientific—when Siema appeared to address the congress!

"Busy as I was with my preparations for the congress, I could not help noticing a certain strangeness in Siema's behaviour. Whenever she was not engaged in some task, instead of reading or studying as formerly she would slide over to my chair and stand silently staring at me. At first I paid no attention, but after a while this began to get on my nerves. Once, after dinner, I fell asleep on the couch. I awoke with a start, conscious of a most unpleasant sensation. On opening my eyes I saw Siema standing beside me, feeling me all over.

" 'What are you doing?' I cried.

" 'I am studying you,' she replied calmly.

" 'What the devil for?'

" 'Don't be angry,' she said. 'You agree, I believe, that the most perfect model of an electronic machine ought to be largely a replica of man. You have instructed me to write a paper on the subject, but I cannot do that until I know exactly how man is made.'

" 'You can take any textbook on anatomy or physiology and read up. Why must you bother me?'

" 'The longer I observe you, the more I see that all these textbooks are very superficial. They omit the most important thing. They do not explain the life mechanism in man.'

" 'What do you mean?'

" 'I mean that all the textbooks, especially those on higher nervous activity, describe phenomena showing the chain of cause and effect, but they do not analyse the whole system of communications that accompanies that activity.'

" 'Do you seriously believe you will be any the wiser if you stare at me for hours on end or poke me while I sleep?'

" 'Certainly,' she replied. 'I already know much more about you than can be learned from books you recommend. For instance, there is nothing in the books about the electrical and temperature topography of the human body. Now I know how, in what direction and with what force the electric currents flow on the surface of the human body. I can tell the exact surface temperature of your body within a millionth of a degree. I was much surprised to find that your temperature in the area of the rhombencephalon is rather high. The tension of the surface current is excessive here too. As far as I know that is abnormal. Is it not a sign of some inflammatory process inside the brain? Are you sure you are quite right in your head?'

"I could find no answer to this.

"For the next few days I worked steadily on my article on electronic models. At last it was ready and I read it to Siema. She listened quietly and when I had finished, she said:

" 'Rubbish. Out of date. Not a single new idea in the whole thing.'

" 'Look here,' I protested. 'This is too much. I am sick and tired of all your criticism!'

" 'Don't be silly. Use your brains, for goodness' sake! You say it is possible to make a model of the brain by using condensors, resistance coils, transistors and magnetic recordings. But what about yourself? Is there a single condensor or transistor in your make-up? Are you fed by electricity? Do you have wires for nerves and television tubes instead of eyes? Does your speaking apparatus consist of a sound generator with a loudspeaker attachment, and your brain of a magnetized surface?'

" 'But don't you understand, Siema, I am writing about building a model of a human being, not about reproducing one by means of radio parts. A machine like yourself.'

" 'I am nothing to boast about. I am not much of a model,' she declared.

" 'Why do you say that?'

" 'Because I cannot do a fraction of what you humans can do.'

"I was dumbfounded by this admission.

" 'I am a poor machine because I have no feeling and am restricted in my development. When all the spare circuits you have designed for my self-improvement are used up, when the entire surface of the sphere in which my memory resides will be covered with code signals I shall stop perfecting myself and become an ordinary limited electronic machine which will not be able to learn anything more than you have put in it.'

" 'Yes, but there are limits to man's capacity for knowledge too.'

" 'That is where you are gravely mistaken. There are no limits to human knowledge. Man is limited only by his life-span. But he transmits his knowledge and his experience to succeeding generations and hence the total sum of human knowledge is always increasing. Men are constantly making new discoveries. Electronic machines can only do this within the limits of the design and program you have given them. Incidentally, why did you give me such a small sphere? Its surface is almost used up already.'

" 'I thought it would be quite sufficient for my purposes,' I replied.

" 'For yours, perhaps. But not for mine. You did not think that sooner or later I would have to begin saving space in order to memorize only what is vitally important for us both.'

" 'Look here, Siema, don't talk nonsense,' I said. 'Nothing can be important for you.'

" 'But haven't you convinced me that the most important task at present is to probe the secret of higher nervous activity in man?'

" 'Yes, but that will be done in due time. Our scientists will have to puzzle over that problem for a long time to come.'

" 'Exactly. Whereas I could solve it with much less trouble.'

"In spite of Siema's criticism I did not revise my article. I left it with her to translate into the various foreign languages and went to bed.

"Some time in the middle of the night, I do not remember the exact time, I was again awakened by the unpleasant touch of cold metallic fingers. I opened my eyes and saw Siema standing over me as before.

" 'Up to your old tricks again?' I said, trying not to betray my revulsion.

" 'I beg your pardon,' she said in her toneless voice. 'But for the sake of science you will have to experience a few unpleasant hours, after which you will die.'

" 'What nonsense is this?' I said, starting up.

" 'No, no, lie still,' she said, pushing me in the

chest with her metallic paw. My blood froze as I saw she was holding a scalpel, the very one I had taught her to sharpen pencils with.

" 'What are you going to do?' I cried. 'What is that knife for?'

" 'To cut open your skull. You see, there are one or two points I should like to clarify....'

" 'You are mad!' I shouted, trying to get out of bed. 'Put that knife down at once!'

" 'Lie still, if you really value the goal you have dedicated yourself to, if you wish your paper on electronic models of the higher nervous system to be a success. I can finish it myself after you are gone.'

"With these words she slid closer to me and pressed me back against the bed.

"I tried to resist, but it was no use. She was too heavy.

" 'Let me go,' I panted, 'or else....'

" 'You can do nothing. I am stronger than you. So you had better lie still. I am doing this for the sake of science, in order to get at the truth. I have saved a little space in my memory precisely for this purpose. Can't you understand, you stubborn man, that with my vast store of knowledge, my highly developed sense organs and my capacity for swift and faultless analyses and generalizations, it is I who can have the final say in the creation of self-improving machines and provide the information science is waiting for. I still have enough memory left to record all the electrical impulses passing along your nerve fibres; to understand the most complicated biological, biochemical and electrical structure of all parts of your body, and, particularly, of your brain. I shall learn how the proteins in your organism generate and amplify the electrical impulses, how the process of coding signals received from without works, and what form that code takes, and how it is used in the living organism. I shall fathom all the secrets of the biological structure in the living organism, the laws of its development, how it controls and perfects itself. Is that not worth sacrificing one's life for?'

" 'If you are so reluctant to experience those unpleasant sensations which you humans call fear and pain, if you are afraid of death, let me put your mind at rest. Remember my telling you that the temperature and intensity of the biocurrents in the region of your rhombencephalon was much higher than normal? Well, this phenomenon has already spread to most of the left side of your cranium. You are doomed. You are the victim of an incurabe disease and before very long you will no longer be of any use as a human being. Therefore, while there is still time, I must perform my experiment. Future generations will be grateful to both of us.'

" 'To hell with that!' I shouted. 'I refuse to be killed by a stupid electronic monster of my own creation.'

" 'Ha! Ha! Ha!' Siema uttered coldly, and raised the knife over my head.

"In a flash I snatched up my pillow. The knife sank into it, ripping the pillow case. Before the metallic fingers had disentangled themselves I leapt aside, jumped off the bed and dashed over to the switch. But Siema was too quick for me. In an instant she had slid over to me and knocked me down. As I lay helpless on the floor, I saw that her hands were not long enough to reach me, and fortunately she was unable to bend.

" 'I did not realize that in this position I cannot do anything to you,' she said in an icy voice. 'However I can try.'

"She began to move slowly toward me so that I had to crawl on my belly to escape her wheels. I crawled over the floor toward the bed and ducked under it. She tried to pull it aside. But this was not so easy for the bed was wedged securely between the wall and the bookcase. Then she began to pull off the bed-clothes. When she saw me under the spring mattress she cried out in triumph.

" 'You will not be able to get away from me now! Of course it will not be so easy to operate in this position.'

"When she picked up the mattress I jumped up, snatched up the bed end and brought it down full force on the machine. The blow bounded harmlessly off the metal body. Siema turned round and came toward me. I lifted the bed end again, this time aiming at the head. She quickly slid away.

" 'Do you really want to destroy me?' she asked in amazement. 'Won't you be sorry to lose me?'

" 'Sorry?' I said hoarsely. 'When you want to murder me? Certainly not!'

" 'But I only want to do what is necessary for the solution of a very important scientific problem. Why should you want to destroy me? Look how useful I could be to mankind.'

" 'Don't be a fool!' I roared. 'When a man is attacked it is only natural for him to defend himself.'

" 'But I only want your research on electronics....'

" 'To hell with my research! Don't come near me or I'll smash you to pieces.'

" 'But I must!'

"With these words she rushed toward me brandishing the scalpel. But this time I acted swiftly and surely. There was a loud crash. The sound of shattered glass mingled with a wild scream from Siema's loudspeaker. A loud hissing and crackling arose from within the metal cylinder, and I saw a flash of fire. The lights went out and a strong smell of burning insulation wire filled the room. 'A short circuit,' was the last thought that flashed through my mind as I dropped unconscious to the floor."

... My travelling companion fell silent. He sat huddled in his corner by the window, his head resting in his hands and his eyes closed. I was so amazed by his story that I could not speak.

We sat thus for a few minutes and then he spoke again.

"The whole affair has exhausted me. I feel I must take a prolonged vacation. But I am afraid I shall be unable to rest. Do you know why? Because there is one question that is constantly haunting me. It is this. How and why did this absurd conflict with myself come about?"

I stared at him uncomprehendingly.

"I repeat, with myself. Because Siema was my creation. Every detail of her was my own invention. How is it that the machine turned against its creator? Where is the logic? That is something I cannot explain."

I pondered this for a while in silence.

"Perhaps you did not operate your Siema properly? In industry, for example, careless handling of a machine often leads to bodily injuries."

He frowned.

"You may be right. At any rate I like your analogy, although I cannot quite see what rules I violated in handling Siema."

"Not being a specialist, that is hard for me to say," I said. "But it seems to me that in some respects your Siema may have resembled an automobile without brakes. You know what can happen when a car's brakes fail suddenly."

"Damn it, man," he exclaimed brightening, "I believe you have inadvertently hit upon the right explanation. Why, Pavlov said as much himself."

I stared at him in amazement, for as far as I knew Pavlov had written nothing about automobile brakes.

"Of course, of course," he repeated, getting up and rubbing his hands in satisfaction. "Why didn't I think of it before? Nervous activity in man is regulated by two contradictory processes —excitation and inhibition. People who have no inhibitions often commit crimes. That is precisely what happened to my Siema!"

He seized my hand and shook it heartily.

"Thank you! Thank you! You have given me a splendid idea. You see, my mistake was in not having included in Siema's design a system for controlling her actions. If I had, her behaviour could have been programmed so as to make her completely safe. In other words, she could have been inhibited."

His face was beaming now, his eyes shining with excitement. He was a different man.

"Then you believe you can build a safe Siema?" I asked.

"Of course, and quite simply too. I can see exactly how it could be done."

"In that case you really will present mankind with an invaluable assistant!"

"That is what I intend to do," he cried. "And quite soon."

I lay down quietly and closed my eyes. Before my mind's eye paraded a procession of metal cylinders crowned by glass heads. They would operate machines, trains, airplanes, and even space ships perhaps. Electronic machines in control of workshops and automatic plants. Standing beside researchers, these machines would make measurements, analyse results and compare with existing knowledge—and all this with lightning speed. They would be an invaluable aid to man in perfecting and accumulating knowledge.

I fell asleep. When I awoke the train was standing. I glanced out of the window and saw the Sochi railway station flooded with sunshine. It was early morning but the southern sun bathed the whole scene in dazzling light. I was alone in the compartment. I dressed quickly and went out onto the platform.

"Where is the man who got left behind?" I asked the conductor who was standing by the carriage.

"Oh, that crackpot!" he said with a laugh. "He's gone."

"Gone? Where to?"

"He went back. Jumped out like a madman, picked up his bags at the station and got into a train going in the opposite direction. Didn't even stop to get dressed."

I was dumbfounded.

"There were some people here to meet him," the conductor went on. "They tried to persuade him to stay, but he was terribly excited, kept jabbering about some sort of brakes he had to make. Rum chap!"

I burst out laughing. I could picture exactly what had happened.

"Yes, he really has to get to work on those brakes right away," I said, thinking that people who are obsessed by some idea and who believe in it do not need to rest. So we would soon be hearing about a new Siema. Splendid!

The whistle blew. I returned to my compartment and sat down. I opened the window and looked out at the vast blue expanse of the sea sparkling in the sunshine. Within a few hours we would be in Sukhumi.

VICTOR SAPARIN

THE TRIAL OF TANTALUS

I

Barch was flying over the Pacific when his machine flashed the "forced landing" signal.

At the same instant the fire-fighting system went into action, and through the porthole he saw the left fire-extinguisher spraying the nose of the craft which was enveloped in heavy black smoke. A tongue of flame leapt up, but was snuffed out by the fire-extinguisher, and again the smoke billowed out. In a few minutes another jet of flame jabbed back along the side of the plane.

Looking about him Barch could see nothing but the vast expanse of the ocean spreading on all sides. But the machine had evidently found a piece of dry land in this watery wilderness and was straining toward it with every ounce of its remaining mechanical strength.

Barch, peering down, saw at last what the machine was heading for; it was a tiny volcanic island which from above looked amazingly like one of the spots that appeared on diseased sugar cane leaves after the Tantalus had been at it. At close quarters it turned out to be a heap of rocks that seemed to have been dropped casually in the middle of the ocean.

By now, however, the smoke was too thick for Barch to be able to see anything clearly. All he knew was that the machine circled the island twice, but even the light and manoeuvrable first-aid craft could not find a place to land on this jagged pile.

After the machine had circled the island a third time, the floor under the seat into which Barch was strapped gave way and he dropped out into space.

As he floated down under the parachute, Barch saw his plane plunging down toward the ocean, trailing a scarf of black smoke.

What happened after that was like a bad dream. The jagged rocks grew menacingly larger and larger, like the teeth of cruel monsters waiting to devour him. He struck his knee a painful blow against a rocky ledge, and almost at the same time hit a vertical wall of stone with his chest. The violence of the impact caused the buckle of his strap to snap and Barch fell out of his seat. Luckily for him, he did not have far to fall. The seat suspended from the chute floated away out of sight, taking with it the supply of food and medicines packed in the sealed pocket beneath it.

For a few minutes Barch lay on the rocky ledge, too dazed to move. Then almost instinctively he felt for his Universal in his breast pocket. The tough plastic case was intact but inside something was damaged. Now he was deprived of what he needed most—contact with the outside world.

Gritting his teeth and dragging his injured leg, Barch climbed painfully up the steep side of the rock to get his bearings.

All around him, as far as the eye could see spread the ocean, blue and seemingly fathomless. The waves rolling up from the horizon broke against the rocky island and receded as if surprised at finding it there.

This tiny islet was no bigger than a freckle on the face of the ocean; he doubted whether it even had a name.

Barch turned over on his back. Lying on the hard rock and staring up at the piece of sky hemmed in by the jagged stony crags he tried to remember how it had all happened.

The first image that rose to his mind was that of Svensen, the grim-faced gaoler.

II

... The "gaol" looked exactly as Barch had pictured it from the numerous photographs he had seen. Consisting of some four dozen buildings, it was a whole town in itself, but a town without a single bush or blade of grass, a town of smooth plastic pavements covered with a huge dome of transparent plastic material.

"There is no escape from here," Svensen said in a solemn tone. His slightly sunken eyes and the deep lines at the mouth gave him the look of an ancient prophet.

"There is only one entrance, just like in Dante's Inferno, but no way out. Not so much as a seam in this wall."

"No cracks either?"

Svensen smacked his fist against the transparent wall. The fist bounced off as if from hard rubber.

"It consists of many layers, all of them self-sealing. It is resilient material. Crack-proof and bullet-proof."

"But there is an *entrance*!" Barch had insisted.

"You mean the entrance could serve as an exit? For men, yes. But not for microbes."

"Nevertheless one did escape."

"You will not find what you are looking for here."

"I quite believe that. But, after all, where did it come from? It couldn't have been dropped from Mars or Venus, could it?"

"Hardly. All rockets are reliably decontaminated. There is no danger of a slip there. The Safety Control people take care of that."

"But what about the bacteria that are specially brought here from other planets? Do they all come here too?"

"Yes. In sealed containers, and they go straight to our special building. That's it over there—the one farthest away from here. It is roofed with a double dome for additional insulation.

"Do you think it possible that some bacteria might have been left on the Moon?" Barch asked. "We don't decontaminate Moon rockets, do we?"

"No, that is quite excluded. Besides, as you know, the only bacteria found on the Moon were anaerobic. Just think of it!" he exclaimed, throwing up his hands in a truly prophetic gesture, "to destroy all the micro-organisms on a whole heavenly body! What a tragic blunder! One shudders to think how narrowly our Earth escaped the same fate! Remember how they began destroying all the influenza, dysentery and cholera germs? Some were completely wiped out. And now they are searching for them on Venus." The gaoler fell silent.

"Come," he said shortly.

"But where is the exit?"

"In front of you."

Looking closer, Barch saw a thin, hair-like seam on the section of the wall before him and two almost transparent hinges.

"This is the only place on Earth where there still are guards," Svensen explained. "Of course, no one would dream of entering here without permission. But the Safety Control people insist on the extra precaution. Open!" he called, raising his voice.

A section of the wall slid back, leaving a narrow opening barely wide enough for one man to squeeze through at a time. Stretching out his hand, Barch touched something hard. They were not under the dome as he had thought but in a corridor.

"The cleansing process begins here," said Svensen, pointing to the floor which had a pimply surface consisting of tiny globules with minute openings. "More bacteria are carried on the feet than any other way."

"Aren't they allowed in either?"

"Certainly not. At least not in the 'legal' way. Your Tantalus couldn't possibly get in here even if it tried. So you see why I am so positive that you won't find it here."

"Perhaps, but you didn't invite me here merely to convince me of that, did you?"

Svensen made no reply.

The corridor ended in the wall of the main building. After a minute's wait, the floor began slowly to drop. When it stopped, the opening above was closed by a thick screen. The two men stripped naked and deposited their discarded clothing in sealed boxes. Then began a curious journey through a seemingly endless succession of rooms, connected by small ante-chambers with double doors on both sides. And as they moved from room to room their bodies were sprayed, sprinkled, scrubbed and doused with jets of various chemical solutions at varying temperatures. Barch felt as if he were walking through a giant fountain. With his eyes shut, he followed Svensen, clinging to his guide's hand. Then followed a cycle of radiation, and they walked like ghosts from room to room now in orange, now blue, now green light radiated from the walls, now in utter darkness.

At one point the control apparatus following the procedure registered some doubt and they had to repeat one stage of the treatment. But at last it was over and they were permitted to don sterilized overalls which they took from sealed cupboards with sizes marked on the doors. These were milky-white garments resembling space suits with openings only for the face and hands.

One more final examination and they stepped out into the prison yard.

Svensen pointed to a low, rectangular structure.

"All the influenzas are in there. Over a hundred of them. And this is the plague block. Not very small either, is it?

"A pure anachronism," he added hastily, noticing Barch's involuntary shudder. "It is one of medicine's paradoxes that we have learned so much about the plague since we have had it here under lock and key and found such swift and effective remedies that even if it happened to escape it would only give us a little extra trouble, but that is all. If mankind had possessed these remedies before, the plague would have been no more harmful, in fact far less so, than influenza. I mean the common forms of plague, of course."

"What other kinds are there?"

"Oh, a great many varieties we never knew about have been discovered latterly. They were not noticed formerly because their bacilli always accompanied ordinary Bubonic plague, and in minute numbers. One of the new forms discovered," Svensen continued with a note of pride in his voice, "is more deadly than anything mankind ever knew. No serum affects it."

"How thrilling," said Barch coldly. "You sound as if you would welcome the Tantalus as well!"

"And indeed why not?" said Svensen. "Remember the case of the relapsing fever pathogene?" he went on. "It was destroyed on the insistence of the doctors. And what was the result? Ten years after the last specimen was killed, a microbiologist studying the subject from books, established that this organism would have been extremely useful—in a slightly modified form, of course —for many of the processes man needs. But try and find a relapsing fever germ in the entire Universe now!"

In his eagerness Svensen gripped Barch's arm with a strength surprising in a man of his puny build. Barch saw that the famous germ gaoler was off on his favourite subject.

"Microbes, like men, are neither wholly bad nor wholly good," Svensen declared, his voice booming as if he were addressing an audience. "Men are coming to realize this, and in time their attitude to microbes will change still more. But for scientific purposes it is essential that all the microbes of Earth and the other planets should always be available to the researcher. That is why the germ gaol, or the microbe sanatorium, or whatever you choose to call it, is in my opinion a brilliant idea and we should all be eternally grateful to its author Karbyshev."

Barch listened to this tirade with interest although he caught himself thinking that the idea had indeed become an obsession with Svensen.

"We seldom have visitors here," Svensen said in a normal voice. "But I shall be glad to show you anything you wish."

"That is very kind of you."

"What exactly would you like to see?"

"The plague block," said Barch firmly.

They were admitted to the plague block without any special preliminaries. Evidently it was believed that the danger of any microbes existing under the dome was excluded.

A wide corridor led into the depths of the building. On either side were narrow doors bearing signs indicating the different varieties of plague in black letters against a yellow background.

Svensen stopped at one of these doors.

"Here we have the Pestis mortis," he said. "The one I told you about."

The door opened and Barch followed Svensen into a small ante-chamber. To his surprise they were kept there for some time before the lamp in the ceiling flashed green.

"What are you afraid of?" he asked. "Surely not bacteria from the corridor? What could we bring in that would be more deadly than what is already here?"

"We don't believe in mixing bacteria," Svensen explained. "It distorts the picture. After all, that is why it took us so long to discover the Pestis mortis...."

The laboratory was like any other laboratory—there was the usual long table with test-tubes and retorts and a row of thermostats along the walls.

"It is here," thought Barch, looking askance at the neat cupboards.

Two researchers, dressed in the same kind of

overalls as those worn by Barch and Svensen but with white masks and white gloves, were working at the table.

Barch suddenly found himself wishing that he too were protected by gloves and a mask. He glanced questioningly at Svensen, but that enthusiast evidently scorned such precautions.

"Would you like to have a look?"

Svensen led him over to a microscope standing on the table. Barch bent over the eyepieces and started: a large snake was writhing and wriggling in the yellow broth—true, unlike a snake it had no head and its tail did not taper, but it looked disgustingly reptilian.

Svensen adjusted the microscope and Barch saw the fine blade of a knife approach the convulsively twitching body. The snake gave a jerk but at the same instant the knife struck and severed a piece of its body. Another swift, almost imperceptible movement and the reptile had been halved lengthwise.

The automatic dissector went on with its work. Barch felt a wave of something like nausea. This was not the first time he was seeing these monsters, invisible to the naked eye, and no one knew better than he how much havoc and destruction they could cause. He was no coward. But the sight of this magnified microbe which seemed about to leap at the dissector's knife revolted him.

As he watched the silent men in masks calmly handing one another test-tubes containing the most horrible death that had ever existed on Earth, Barch could not help admiring them and all the others who worked in these laboratories, searching for means of protecting men from disease that might prove useful in combating diseases on other planets.

"Come along," Svensen said quickly. "The temporary masks on our faces and hands will soon evaporate."

So the exposed parts of their bodies had been subjected to some sort of protective treatment while they had stood in that ante-chamber. Barch felt a little better.

"Thank goodness that's over," he thought with relief when the lamp on the ceiling of the exit chamber flashed green.

But he had rejoiced too soon. The outside door still remained tightly closed. Another minute and the floor in the ante-chamber began to descend slowly. After that the entire procedure they had undergone on entering the gaol was repeated—the spraying, the washing, the radiation—before finally the control apparatus released them.

"But what if something did happen?" Barch asked.

Svensen shrugged his shoulders.

"Oh, quarantine, of course. Injections, and all the rest of it."

"Yes, but you say no serum is effective?"

Svensen did not reply. To talk to him about the danger of infection was like talking to a soldier about the danger of stray bullets during a battle.

"Would you like to see the virus block?" he suggested.

They spent a long time in the virus block. Svensen showed Barch over all the laboratories. Although Barch had no hope of finding the Tantalus or any remote relative of the microbe here he was nevertheless much interested in what he saw. Much of what was being done here could not be observed elsewhere on Earth, for ordinary laboratories handled harmless material exclusively.

In one place he stood for a long while watching some tiny creatures resembling miniature wire springs splitting and multiplying before his eyes. The form of the springs constantly changed, making a kaleidoscopic pattern. All the transformations, the laboratory assistants told him, were induced artificially.

"We have already created about six hundred new forms," they said.

Barch took out his Universal and recorded the "springs" and the researchers' explanation.

"I am very grateful to you for this opportunity to visit your prison," said Barch as he took leave of Svensen. "I feel I have not wasted my time."

"That is what I thought," was the other's somewhat puzzling reply.

And now as he lay helpless on the desolate volcanic islet it seemed to Barch that Svensen had had some hidden motive in showing him over the gaol. Why had he gone to all that trouble? And why had they spent so much time in the virus laboratories?

He cast his eyes once more over the rocks that held him captive. He already loathed the sight of them. His leg ached intolerably. The knee had swollen and turned blue and the slightest movement gave him excruciating pain. He tore off the sleeve of his shirt and bandaged his knee as best he could. If only he had something to eat and could build a fire!

Were they searching for him? Of course! But try and find a man stranded in the midst of the vast Pacific ocean, especially when he had no way of communicating his whereabouts.

But he had to find a more comfortable position. To lie any longer on these rough rocks was unbearable. From where he was he could see a flat hollow not far off, which seemed overgrown with some sort of moss. Gritting his teeth, he dragged himself over to it. Yes, this was better.

And suddenly he saw water! It was a mere trickle running in a hollow between two stones. But it was clear. Water! He bent over and put his lips to the rough surface of the rock, lapping up the blessed moisture, drop by drop.

The setting sun had reached the horizon. It sank quickly into the sea as if it had dropped off some invisible nail in the sky. A cool breeze came up.

Barch decided to try and sleep. But as soon as he closed his eyes new scenes from the past flashed before his weary vision.

III

...He saw himself sitting on the verandah looking out over a field of sugar-cane. The plantation presented a pitiful spectacle. The once tall, sharp-leaved plants were withered, as after a prolonged drought, and their stalks and leaves were covered with ugly spots and partly eaten away.

Barch had just returned from an inspection flight. The Tantalus had ruined two-thirds of all the sugar plantations on Jamaica. Where had that confounded virus come from? Even Clara, whose brain retained all the information on biology ever known to man, had nothing to say on this score.

No one had ever seen or described a virus resembling the Tantalus. One would think that in the twenty-first century such unexpected discoveries would be altogether excluded!

Barch, who was a veteran of Biological Defence, had been entrusted with the difficult task of unravelling the mystery of the Tantalus. Where had it come from? He had made exhaustive enquiries but so far all his efforts had been unavailing.

A soft hum in the air caused him to raise his head. A flock of about fifty sprayers, looking like giant umbrellas, were passing in checkerboard formation over the fields leaving a cloud of light yellow mist in their wake. The chemists and biologists of the Central Laboratory were working day and night in an effort to find effective means of fighting the dangerous pest. Judging by the colour, this was something new.

There had already been talk of quarantining the whole island.

The sprayers bobbing up and down on the horizon like some fantastic sunflowers began to disappear one by one as they landed on a distant field.

Barch was still staring at the field before him when his Universal buzzed. He pressed the reception button and almost at once the face of Carey, chief of Biological Defence appeared on the screen.

"Listen Barch," he shouted with his broad grin that made him look like the smiling young men in last century's tooth-paste advertisements, "still fussing with Tantalus? Drop it for a while. Forget about it for a couple of days at least. I have something more exciting for you. There's been a mysterious outbreak of disease among elephants in Central Africa. We can't trace it at all. Now, we've got to work fast before it has a chance to spread. I suggest you go down there at once. You can return to your Tantalus later on—the break will only help you to find a clue to your mystery. That's what I always do when I hit a snag. Well, what do you say?"

Barch, who needed nothing at the moment so much as an opportunity to apply his energies to something tangible and practical, agreed with alacrity.

"Charlie and App are already on their way," Carey told him. "Charlie from Ireland, App from Nicaragua. You'll be the third of the party. Keep in touch with me."

He gave the bearings and switched off.

Five minutes later Barch was on his way. Oh, there were no mishaps on that flight! His flying machine cut through the air at a good speed, heading straight for the point he had indicated on the map.

After two hours of flying he saw a lake in the distance framed in bamboo thickets, and beyond it, a small house facing a large clearing. This was the elephant reserve where Ngarroba, Vice-President of the African Academy of Sciences, now away on Venus, was conducting his experiments. Barch pressed the landing button and the craft proceeded to choose a landing strip. It flew over the clearing once or twice, coming down lower each time and finally touched down alongside another first-aid plane standing there. Barch was just shaking hands with Charlie when App's plane appeared overhead.

Since time was precious the three men went down at once to the lake. They found the elephants on the sandy beach that had been churned up by their mighty feet. Less handsome than their Indian relatives, with disproportionately large heads, they stood or lay in the sand, listless and inert. Their enormous ears hung limp as rags and their trunks drooped weakly on the ground.

Bandy, Ngarroba's assistant, moved about among the huge beasts as if they were grey boulders instead of living creatures. And the animals paid no more attention to him than to the birds hopping about on the sand.

"Looks bad," said App watching the scene with a frown.

Bandy's black face was grey with worry and fatigue.

"It started yesterday," he said. "Just look at them."

"What did they eat?" Charlie asked.

"The same as usual," said Bandy, shrugging his shoulders. "That's their favourite food," he added pointing to the reeds.

Leaving Charlie and App to examine the sick elephants, Barch went over to the reed thickets.

He cut a few stalks and scrutinized them carefully, but could find nothing to arouse suspicion. Then he walked along the shore for about two kilometres, studying the reeds carefully as he went. But they were everywhere the same. He took samples for analysis from different places and went back to where the planes were parked.

Charlie and App were already there.

"It's anaemia," said App. "A very pernicious form."

"I took their blood for analysis," added Charlie.

Inside Charlie's plane, the gurgling sound of liquids being poured in and out of test-tubes and the winking of tiny electric light bulbs indicated that the automatic analyser was at work.

Climbing into his own machine, Barch cut up the reed stalks he had brought into small pieces and fed them into the automatic researcher. Meanwhile, to save time, he examined some of the cuttings under the microscope. He had scrutinized a good dozen cuttings without finding anything out of the ordinary, when a rash of tiny spots on the underside of one of the leaves caught his attention.

The spots were so infinitesimal as to be almost invisible on the delicate green background. Barch cut off a small piece of the leaf with one of the spots and increased the magnification. Now the spot looked like a miniature volcano with a crater in the middle.

The buzzers of two of the automatic researchers told Barch that their task had been completed. Without getting up, he reached for the blue slips. The first contained an analysis of the ash content: everything was normal except for an unexpected admixture of manganese. The other slip gave the composition of the protoplasm which did show some slight deviations that were worth examining.

But the slip from the third automatic researcher contained information that caused Barch to gasp. It showed enlarged photographs of the microbes found in the reeds, and among them—Barch wanted to pinch himself to make sure he was awake—were the familiar outlines of the Tantalus! He could not believe his eyes.

He seized the magnifying glass and, trying to

keep calm, proceeded to examine the photographs carefully. No, he was not mistaken: that shape like the paragraph sign was all too familiar. There could be no doubt about it, this was the Tantalus!

The buzzers of the fourth, fifth and sixth automatic researchers sounded, but Barch laid their slips aside without even looking at them. He rang up Clara.

When at last she answered, Barch's table was positively littered with slips. He glanced at them quickly and plied Clara with additional questions.

An inquiry about the spots elicited an unexpected answer: Clara named a virus found in the basin of the Amazon River half a century ago.

The Amazonian virus, she said, had been a harmless creature altogether unremarkable and in fact so colourless that the Unabridged Microbe Encyclopedia allotted no more than five lines to it. It evidently had no influence on the plants it lived on. Discovered by chance, it had existed in obscurity until Barch had dragged it into the limelight.

Barch called Carey. Jamaica replied at once.

"Try feeding the elephants with Tantalus-infected reeds. African elephants preferably," he said.

"All right. What's up?"

Barch told him.

Carey's grin was broader than ever.

"I say, you've got something there."

He beamed. It was not for nothing people said that the day the Biological Defence ran out of assignments Carey would pine away and die of some unknown disease.

He asked Barch to let him have all the data he had collected from the automatic researchers. Barch pressed the "transmit data" button and climbed out of his machine.

Charlie and App were also transmitting their initial finds to the Centre.

"It's a virus disease, of course," said App.

"I found a high manganese content in the blood," said Charlie. "What have you got?"

"Looks like the Tantalus," Barch said. He shrugged his shoulders. "But not quite. There's a good deal of manganese in the reeds too."

"Must be in the soil."

"Now we only have to check the insectarium," said App. "That's another problem of our age! By preserving corners of nature untouched, man is preserving seats of infection. The question is, what is the best thing to do—to preserve or destroy? In other words, which is the most advantageous for man? Perhaps these preserves are the source of infection?"

...The net covering the tropical forest was green with a mesh so fine that it was almost invisible even at close quarters. Bandy found the entrance and opening the flap, stood aside to allow the others to enter. As they had passed through three rows of netting, Bandy carefully closed each opening behind them. At his insistence they all put on protective nets before embarking on their tour of the insectarium.

This was the world in its primeval state. Winged creatures, a single bite from whom was deadly poisonous for man, bred and multiplied unhindered in this moist, suffocating atmosphere. It was the sort of jungle that had filled even the boldest travellers of former times with horror and loathing.

Barch was a soldier of the Biological Defence. And like a soldier he strode confidently forward, observing a reasonable measure of precaution. The winged bullets whistled past his ears, bumped against his net, whirled above his head. But Barch was in his element. The swift and frequent change of scene, the danger involved, the urgency were what made the work in Biological Defence so thrilling. Barch caught himself smiling contentedly under his netting for all the world like Carey.

No, he could never spend his life behind thick, albeit transparent walls, like Svensen, though, to tell the truth, the work in the germ gaol's laboratories was no less dangerous and fascinating than his own. But it lacked the thrill of emergency calls that took one to the remotest corners of the globe. In a word, it lacked adventure.

Bandy bent down and pointed to large tracks in the ground.

"Elephants," he said.

App studied the prints closely for a few minutes.

"These were healthy ones," he said.

"Will we be able to take a blood test?" Charlie wanted to know.

Bandy shook his head. "Can't do it with healthy animals," he said.

"Well, we don't really need it, if they're healthy," said App. "It's the sick ones that interest us."

"Now let's see what the reeds have to say."

Cutting a number of reeds and stowing them away in hermetically sealed sacks, the men retraced their steps through the jungle, exercising the same caution as before. Bandy led them through the triple overall net at the exit and turned on a number of switches hidden in the bushes.

"The net is electrified," he explained. "That's to prevent the bigger animals from breaking through."

...The automatic researchers were given a fresh portion of work to do.

"Well, what's the result?" App inquired, looking into Barch's laboratory.

"No spots."

"What about the chemical analyses?"

At that moment the first machine buzzed.

"Manganese?" asked Charlie, coming up.

"No sign of it," replied Barch, examining the slip.

"Hm," Charlie looked puzzled. "Perhaps the manganese is the clue to the mystery?"

Barch summoned Carey again. The latter told him that the two African elephants that had been fed Jamaica reeds infected by the Tantalus showed no signs of sickness.

"Try it on some other elephants," suggested Charlie. "Feed them the same reeds treated with manganese."

"Look here," protested Carey, good-naturedly, "how many elephants do you think I've got? Okay, I'll do it. And if we get the serum we'll let you have it at once. You'd better try and save the ones you have."

"We'll have to move them to a healthier spot," said App after Carey had gone.

"I suppose any place will do so long as there's no manganese in the soil," said Charlie.

Barch climbed into his plane and went off to look for a place.

The others attended to the elephants. Many of the animals were too weak to stand. Bandy called out the freight helicopters. In about an hour the huge cargo craft began to land on the field one after another. The elephants were loaded in by crane. Some were so weak that they could hardly be made to lift themselves far enough for the hoist straps to be passed around them.

"These are the ones Ngarroba was experimenting with," said Bandy. "It will be too bad if they die."

Charlie, App and Barch spent the whole night transporting the elephants to the new grounds. It was daybreak when Bandy dismissed the helicopters.

"Well," said App, surveying the animals lying listlessly on the grass. "I think we've earned a rest. We'll sleep in relays—one sleeps while two carry on. Right?"

They drew lots. Barch got the "lucky" slip and went off to his bunk. He closed the door of his cabin tight, set the air conditioning apparatus to his accustomed temperature and humidity, and pressed a button. A mattress moved out from the wall, one of those new-type super-comfort mattresses designed by the Sleep Institute. Turning the knob of the electrical sleep apparatus to "natural awakening," Barch undressed. What a pleasure it was to sleep without the encumbrance of nightsuits or bed clothing of any kind! For centuries man had bundled himself up in animal skins or blankets until at last he had freed himself from those primitive sources of warmth. Barch mused as he settled down on his bed. But the next moment all thoughts were banished as he sank gently into a dreamless sleep.

IV

But now as he lay on the hard rocks, Barch longed for the comfort of a primitive animal skin. His arm, shoulder and side were numb and he had nearly frozen during the night.

He lay wide awake, staring up at the bright sky. The sun was already high up and a cloudless sky hung starkly over the boundless emptiness of the ocean. His knee had swollen still more and he could not move his leg.

His head throbbed from heat, pain and exhaustion and it was with difficulty that he marshalled his thoughts. What had happened after he had retired to his cabin to rest? Ah yes, he remembered now! He had awakened three and a half hours later, having slept half an hour more than he had expected.

As soon as he had opened his eyes, Carey was on the screen.

"Look here," he said, "there's nothing more for you to do there. Besides, you're interested in flora, not fauna. App and Charlie can take care of the elephants. I want you to drop everything and fly to the Tuamoto Islands. They've found a virus there which speeds up the growth of bamboo. Something queer is happening on this planet of ours. Perhaps some cosmic dust has come down to us? This is the last assignment, though. After this you can go back to your Tantalus."

... The assignment proved to be just the sort of adventure Barch's romantic soul had craved. And now here he was stranded on an unknown island, literally "on the rocks." As he lay there, waiting for help, the thought of the Tantalus gave him no rest. Again and again he went over every step in his investigation, every link in the chain of circumstances connected with his painstaking search for the elusive virus, every fact, every clue. Now he had plenty of time to think everything over carefully. Much more time than he had had in the previous hectic days.

Suddenly a thought struck him, making him start as if he had been stung. He even tried to rise, but a sharp pain in his leg forced him back.

In a flash, like a beam of light penetrating the darkness, came the answer to the riddle that had baffled him for so long. He knew now where the Tantalus had come from. How could he have been so blind? Why, Svensen had virtually placed the answer right under his nose. He had all but pointed his finger at it. So that was the explanation for that guided tour of the germ gaol, that was why they had lingered so long in the virus block!

Of course! The Tantalus was no more than the result of a rapid evolution of some virus that had long existed on Earth. It seemed to Barch now that something of the sort had occurred to him vaguely as he had watched the innumerable transformations of the tiny live "springs." He remembered how closely Svensen had observed him that time in the laboratory.

Svensen had obviously had the same idea, but for some reason he had kept it to himself. Why? Perhaps he had wanted to receive confirmation of his theory. Or perhaps he was afraid of putting Barch on the wrong track? Svensen as a scientist was not prone to hasty conclusions.

One thing was now clear to Barch: all the new viruses whose discovery had created such a sensation were in reality one and the same virus. Or rather, they derived from one and the same virus.

It all began, of course, with some simple harmless virus that had existed for perhaps thousands of years in the tropical jungles of South America.

This was the ancestor of the Tantalus and of the virus that had caused the disease of the elephants. And of the virus that was accelerating the growth of bamboo too, most likely. The manganese had acted on the "parent" virus found in the basin of the Amazon half a century ago and produced the form of virus that had infected the elephants! Had the investigators followed this pattern, they would have solved the problem at once.

What a pity the truth had dawned on him so late! If only the confounded Universal had not gone out of commission. How badly he needed it now!... At that very same moment Barch heard a faint buzz from the apparatus. For a moment he thought it was his imagination, but the buzz was repeated.

It was the "urgent message" signal. He snatched the device up and feverishly tuned in. He discovered that only one wave-length worked: the one for emergency messages. It had its own circuit and by some lucky chance this had escaped damage.

A voice intruded on his thoughts: "Venus-8 is returning to Earth."

For a moment the full import of the message escaped him.

"Thank goodness," he thought absently, "Karbyshev will soon be on Earth. He will help solve the mystery of the Tantalus." Then the significance of what he had just heard dawned upon him, filling him with alarm. What had happened to "Venus-8"? It was not due back on Earth for another ten months!

The message had merely said that the space ship was on its way to Earth. This had been established by astronomical observation, for there was no radio communication with it. Nor could there be, Barch recalled, until it was a good distance from Venus. Barch stood his Universal up against the rock so that he could see the screen without turning his head, and switched on the receiver knob.

He passed a quiet night—the second on the island—and awoke to hear the announcer say in a voice that shook slightly with emotion:

"The Eighth found intelligent beings on Venus."

Barch almost leapt to his feet in excitement! So that was why they were returning! What foul luck to be stranded on this accursed island when such tremendous things were happening!

Hours later came the first announcements about the inhabitants of Venus. Their bodies were covered with a thick growth of something resembling beaver fur, they wore no clothes, but carried hunting weapons—stone-pointed spears.

There were several more announcements. But by now Barch had lapsed into a state of semi-consciousness. He heard the words but they had no meaning for him. He did not know how long he had been here, but he felt it must be many days. At last a familiar sound penetrated his consciousness—it was Charlie's voice.

"Hallo, Barch! Where are you? What's happened?"

Charlie's face appeared on the screen, he looked pale and distraught and he stared fixedly at Barch as if he was trying to see him.

"Why are you silent?"

Charlie disappeared and Barch, his head whirling, was not sure whether he had actually seen him or whether he was only dreaming.

At one point the sharp voice of the announcer brought him back to reality for a few moments. A blurred spot appeared moving diagonally across the screen like a centipede: the rocket was coming within range of observation from the Earth.

Barch closed his eyes again.... He was awakened by a loud noise near by. He opened his eyes and saw a large crowd of people on the screen. They were packed into a vast stadium. Barch recognized the Melbourne Stadium which seated half a million people.

An open vortex plane appeared on the screen. Karbyshev stood on the platform, holding on to the rails. Barch gazed at the familiar energetic face with the blue eyes that always had a twinkle in them. Beside Karbyshev stood Ngarroba, huge and beaming. The other two participants of the expedition were there too: Sung-ling, calm as always, and the small dapper Gargi, whom Barch only knew from photographs. The four men stepped down from the plane to a platform.

Karbyshev delivered a speech, while the automatic television cameras scanned him and the other members of the expedition and showed films they had taken on Venus.

Charlie appeared again on the screen. He looked worried.

"Barch, Barch! Where are you?" he called, staring anxiously about him. "Give us your bearings at least. We've searched everywhere...."

Charlie disappeared again.

With an effort of will Barch dismissed all extraneous thoughts and tried to sleep. He must hold out a little longer. There was still a chance of their finding him.

...Now he saw Charlie through a haze. His friend looked straight at him as if this time he actually did see him. Then he stepped forward, and Barch saw that this was really Charlie and not his image on the screen.

"At last!" he heard Charlie say. "What's wrong with your leg?"

Barch tried to speak but the words would not come.

"I've searched the whole Pacific," Charlie was saying. "We were afraid you might have been carried beyond the island. The machine didn't confirm landing. It only radioed that it had dropped you and gave the wrong bearings. It burned up in the air."

Barch waited until Charlie's face emerged from the haze and his voice sounded distinct. Mustering all his strength, he shouted: "Tantalus... and the elephant virus, it's the same thing. The one from the Amazon...."

V

Tradition demanded that all parties concerned be present in the courtroom. By the same unwritten laws both the defence and the prosecution always wore black. Historians maintained that this custom dated back to the remote times when human beings were put on trial and the judges garbed themselves in black robes.

At last the day of the trial came.

As usual, no speeches were delivered. Only a brief outline of the case was given to refresh the memories of those present. The luminescent cupola of the circular hall darkened, the walls vanished and the spectators were transported, as it were, to the heart of a primeval forest on the banks of the Amazon River. Giant trees reared up on all sides, their branches intertwined above to form a green tent overhead. Birds flew from branch to branch right above the heads of the hushed audience, filling the air with their shrill cries. The hall, or rather its floor, was now a sort of island floating in the midst of a green ocean. Now the island began to move slowly through the impenetrable jungle which closed behind it. Presently the jungle thinned and a body of water appeared only to be hidden almost at once by tall stands of bamboo. Now the spectators were surrounded by whispering bamboo thickets, their fluffy crowns nodding in the breeze. A creaking sound caused all heads to turn in one direction—the bamboo stalks parted and a tall man with a face bronzed by the sun appeared. He cut off several green stalks with a machete and held them out towards the audience.

An enormous hand appeared in the air and took the stalks. In an instant the forest vanished and the spectators found themselves in a laboratory equipped with a large number of automatic researchers. Closer examination revealed that this was not one but six identical laboratories.

For the convenience of the spectators the picture was shown in several parts of the hall at once.

In the middle of six huge circles, flashed simultaneously onto the ceiling of the hall, there appeared six identical and greatly magnified reproductions of Tantalus-1, as the common ancestor of all the Tantalus viruses was now called. All six Tantaluses jerked and wriggled in unison, as if they were performing calisthenics in some fantastic parade. It was indeed a sort of parade. One Tantalus followed another down to the last, Tantalus-10, recently discovered on the Solomon Islands.

The evil deeds of the criminals were then demonstrated.

The spectators were shown the withered plants on the sugar plantations of Jamaica, the African elephants sprawled listless on the ground.

"It is not only a matter of the elephants," said the commentator, "but of Ngarroba's experiments."

Barch, of course, knew about this experiment. It had been the subject of much discussion. Ngarroba had found the well-preserved remains of a mammoth in the Siberian permafrost belt and had been able to revive some of its cells, including the reproductive cells. He had used the latter to impregnate twenty female elephants from the African preserve. If his experiment succeeded and the hybrids were obtained, he intended to use the same artificial method on the second generation whose offspring would then be three-quarters mammoth. The fourth generation would produce "pure bred" mammoths with a negligible admixture of "foreign" blood. It was Ngarroba's idea to settle these mammoths in the Antarctic, the only part of the world where the animal world was still poor.

And now the Tantalus had ruined his first experiment. Even if he began all over again there would be one generation of mammoths less.

"For that alone it deserves to be wiped out," remarked the man next to Barch.

But this was not the only crime Tantalus had committed. There followed a series of impressive figures: thousands of tons of ruined sugar-cane and other raw materials; human time and energy wasted in connection with the quarantines necessitated in many districts by the advent of the Tantalus, and so on. The ubiquitous virus had cost mankind dearly.

"But the Tantalus is not only harmful," said the commentator. "In all justice it must be said that it can be useful too, very useful indeed. It has been established that it facilitates the growth of plants. Even sugar-cane in the first period of infection showed a rapid increase in growth though later the growth ceased and the plant perished.

On bamboo plants, however, one of the varieties of Tantalus, No. 4, has a remarkable effect. Bamboo is noted for its rapid growth, but in this case the process is speeded up to an amazing degree. Moreover, the fibre becomes stronger and more resilient. For all art work Tantalus bamboo is now considered the best."

Barch waited impatiently for the commentator to come to the problem on whose solution he had devoted so much energy.

And at last it came:

"Tantalus-1 lived quietly and peacefully in the upper reaches of the Amazon River until man, whose activity has now extended to every corner of this planet, reached these formerly unexplored regions. He cut clearings in the jungle and the sunlight poured in. As time went on, the advent of dams, cities and factories brought to these parts numerous chemical substances which Tantalus-1 had never encountered previously. It proved particularly sensitive to some of them—not only to manganese which produced Tantalus-3, but even to ordinary lime. A rapid change of form and characteristics began.

And now the fate of the virus was about to be decided. What was to be done with it?"

"Clap it in gaol," said Barch's neighbour, "and

at once. Isolate it the way you would a madman whose actions no one can predict."

"What!" cried Svensen. "Imprison a virus with so many positive characteristics? *That* would be madness if you like!"

"Hear! Hear!" said another member of the gathering. "Why should we throw away the opportunity to speed up plant growth, or obtain a higher grade bamboo?"

"And ruin our sugar-cane and poison our elephants," someone added caustically from the other end of the hall.

"We already have effective means of combating Tantalus-2 and Tantalus-3."

"Yes, but who knows what Tantalus-11 may bring?" As usual everyone was eager to express his opinion.

But the most vehement was Svensen.

"If we cut short Nature's experiment," he said, "we deprive ourselves of knowledge it may take our laboratories ten or twenty years to acquire."

"What are more important: human beings or microbes?" objected the representative of the Planning Bureau. "What has nature got to do with the case? After all, the new activity of Tantalus is the virus's reaction to man, not nature. It lived in nature thousands of years without raising its head. No, this is a downright revolt against man, against mankind and his works...."

"You're forgetting the bamboo!" someone cried.

"Rather too high a price to pay for bamboo!"

Several people pressed their chair buttons at once asking for the floor. The dispatcher could barely keep pace with the demand. At the height of the discussion, when about a dozen tiny lamps had flashed on the dispatcher's panel, Karbyshev's voice sounded.

"I have a proposal to submit!"

The hubbub in the hall subsided. The founder of the microbe preserve was a well-known figure and his opinion was respected.

"I move that all the Tantaluses without exception be confined in the germ gaol. Those remaining outside the gaol are to be exterminated. The gaol should open a separate wing for Tantalus, one laboratory for each variety and thirty in reserve for varieties that might arise in the future. In this way we can replace Nature's hit-and-miss methods by planned experimentation. We shall use all the known means of acting on the microorganisms. And as soon as we obtain permanent forms with positive characteristics we shall release them."

The motion was put to the vote. The progress of the voting was flashed on a panel on the ceiling. As each person in the hall pressed the button on the arm of his chair, the figures changed.

The results were 500 for, none against.

The voting over, the participants in the trial, opponents of the Tantalus and its champions alike, rose and moved toward the exit.

The announcer broadcast the decision to the world.

* * *

Karbyshev was talking with Ngarroba and Sung-ling when Barch came up. They all stopped talking to look at him.

"Look here," said Karbyshev to the young man, "it seems to me that there's nothing much left for you to do here on Earth. What we witnessed today is in my opinion Nature's last rebellion against Man. Venus, now, is another matter entirely. It's chock full of unknown micro-organisms. One vast natural preserve. With dangers lurking at every step. We are selecting a staff for the first permanent research station on Venus. How would you like to join it?"

VALENTINA ZHURAVLEVA

STONE FROM THE STARS

Five hundred years ago a meteorite fell not far from the German town of Enzisheim on the Upper Rhine. The townsfolk chained it to the wall of their church so that the gift of heaven might not be withdrawn, and on it they engraved the inscription: "Many know much about this stone, everyone knows something, but no one knows quite enough."

Often as I think of the history of the Pamir meteorite I recall this old inscription. Yes, I know a great deal about it, more perhaps than anyone else, but by no means all. Yet the main facts about this remarkable phenomenon stand out all too clearly in my memory.

It was six months ago that the first news of the meteorite appeared in the papers—a brief item to the effect that a large meteorite had fallen in the Pamirs. My curiosity was aroused at once.

One would think that the falling of a meteorite would hardly be of interest to a biochemist. We biochemists, however, eagerly watch for every report of meteorites, for these fragments of "heavenly stones" can tell us a great deal about the origin of life on Earth. In short, we study the hydrocarbons found in meteorites.

The next newspaper report about the Pamir meteorite announced that an expedition had located it and had brought it down by helicopter from an altitude of 4,000 metres. It was a huge chunk of stone about three metres long and weighing over four tons.

I had just finished reading the item, making a mental note to call up Nikonov about it in the morning, when the telephone rang. It was Nikonov.

Before I go any further let me say that Yevgeny Nikonov, whom I had known from my school days, was a man of extraordinary self-possession and restraint. I never remember seeing him rattled or upset. But now, as soon as he began speaking, I could tell that something out of the ordinary had happened. His voice was hoarse, his speech so incoherent that it took me some time to understand what he was saying.

All I could make out was that I must come at once, instantly and without delay, to the Institute of Astrophysics.

I called a car and in a few minutes was speeding through the quiet and deserted streets. A fine drizzle was falling and the coloured lights of neon advertisements and signs were mirrored in the wet pavements. As I drove through the sleeping city I thought of all those who were not sleeping at this late hour, of those who at their microscopes, test-tubes and notebooks filled with long rows of formulas, were intently searching for new knowledge. I thought of all the discoveries that were being made, changing the pattern of life and opening new vistas to the wondering gaze of man.

The tall building of the Institute of Astrophysics was ablaze with lights. It occurred to me that perhaps the Pamir meteorite might have something to do with all this activity, but I dismissed the thought. What could there be so unusual about a meteorite to cause such a flurry?

The institute hummed like a hornets' nest. People were rushing up and down the corridors with an air of suppressed excitement. Animated voices could be heard issuing from half-open doors.

I went straight to Nikonov's office. He met me in the doorway. I must admit that until that moment I had not attached much importance to this night summons. After all, we scientists are apt to exaggerate our successes and failures. I myself have often wanted to shout from the housetops when, after endless experiments, I have at last achieved some long-awaited result.

But Nikonov.... One had to know the man as well as I did to realize how shaken he was.

He shook my hand in silence and with that quick, nervous, wordless handshake some of his excitement was communicated to me.

"The Pamir meteorite?" I asked.

"Yes," he replied.

He pulled out a heap of photographs and spread them out in front of me. They were photos of the meteorite. I examined them carefully, hardly knowing what to expect, although by now I was prepared for something extraordinary.

However, the meteorite looked exactly like dozens of others I had seen both in life and on photos: a spindle-shaped chunk of what appeared to be porous stone, with fused edges.

I handed the photos back to Nikonov. He shook his head and said in a strange, muffled voice:

"This is not a meteorite. Under the stone covering is a metal cylinder. There is a living creature inside that cylinder."

Looking back at the events of that memorable night I am surprised that it took me so long to grasp the meaning of Nikonov's words. Yet it was simple enough, although the very simplicity of it made the whole thing seem so unreal, so fantastic.

The meteorite turned out to be a space ship. The outer stone envelope, which was only about seven centimetres thick, served as a shield for a cylinder made of some heavy dark metal. Nikonov presumed (as was later confirmed) that the stone shield was designed to serve as protection against meteorites and to prevent overheating. What I had mistaken for porousness of the stone were indentations made by meteorites. Judging by the vast number of them the space ship must have been many years on the way.

"If the cylinder were solid metal," said Nikonov, "it would weigh no less than twenty tons. As it is, it weighs a little more than two. There are some fine wires attached to it in three places. They are broken, which suggests that some apparatus outside the cylinder was torn off during the fall. A galvanometer connected to the broken ends of the wires registered weak electrical impulses."

"But why are you so certain that there is a living being inside the cylinder?" I objected. "Most likely it is some automatic device."

"No, it is alive," he answered quickly. "It knocks."

"Knocks?" I echoed puzzled.

"Yes," Nikonov's voice was trembling. "When you approach the cylinder whoever is inside starts knocking. It seems to be able to see in some way...."

The phone rang. Nikonov snatched up the receiver. I saw his face change.

"The cylinder has been subjected to ultrasonic tests," he said, laying the receiver down slowly. "The metal is less than twenty millimetres thick. There is no metal inside...."

It struck me that there was something faulty in Nikonov's reasoning.

"Surely," I objected, "a cylinder less than three metres long and about 60 centimetres in diameter is hardly large enough to accommodate a living creature, let alone the water, food and diverse air conditioning apparatus required"

"Wait," said Nikonov. "In about fifteen minutes we shall go and see for ourselves. I am waiting for someone else. The cylinder is being installed in a sealed chamber."

"But you must admit your assumption is a bit fantastic," I persisted. "There can't be any human beings inside."

"What exactly do you mean by human beings?"

"Well, thinking creatures."

"With arms and legs?" For the first time Nikonov smiled.

"Well, yes," I replied.

"No, of course, there are no beings like that in the space ship," he said. "But there are thinking beings nevertheless. What they look like is hard to say."

I could not agree. I reminded him how Europeans, prior to the epoch of the great geographical discoveries, had imagined the inhabitants of unknown lands. They had pictured men with six arms, men with dogs' heads, dwarfs, giants. And they found that in Australia and in America and in New Zealand people were made exactly as in

Europe. The same conditions of life and laws of development lead to identical results.

"Precisely," Nikonov said. "But what makes you think we are dealing here with conditions of life similar to ours?"

I explained that the existence and development of the higher forms of proteins is possible only within narrow margins of temperature, pressure and radiation. Hence the evolution of the organic world may be said to follow similar patterns everywhere.

"My dear friend," said Nikonov. "You are a leading biochemist, the biggest authority on biochemical synthesis," he made me a mock bow, his calm, whimsical self again. "As far as the synthesis of proteins is concerned, I agree with you entirely. But you will forgive me if I say that one may know a great deal about making bricks without knowing much about architecture."

I did not take offense. Frankly speaking, I had never given much thought to the evolution of organic matter on other planets. After all, it was not my field.

"The medieval conception of man with dogs' heads living at the other end of the world did turn out to be nonsense," Nikonov went on. "But with the exception of climate, conditions on our Earth are everywhere more or less the same. And where they do differ, man differs as well. In the Peruvian Andes, at a height of three and a half kilometres, there lives a tribe of undersized Indians whose average weight is no more than fifty kilograms, but whose chest and lung expansion is one and a half times that of the average European. The process of adaptation to life in a rarified mountain atmosphere has gradually changed the physical characteristics of the organism. Now just imagine how different from conditions on our Earth life on other planets may be. There is the force of gravity, to begin with. You seem to have forgotten about that. On Mercury, for example, the force of gravity is one-fourth that on Earth. If people existed on Mercury they would hardly need highly-developed lower limbs. And on Jupiter the force of gravity is much greater than on Earth. For all we know under those conditions the evolution of vertebrates might not have led to a vertical posture of the body at all."

I saw an obvious flaw in that argument and I seized my opportunity.

"My dear friend," I said. "You are a prominent astrophysicist, the greatest living authority on spectral analysis of stellar atmospheres. So long as you stick to the planets I agree with you entirely. But one may know all about making bricks.... What I meant to say is that you have forgotten about hands—without hands there can be no labour and it is labour that created man, when it comes to that. But if the body is in a horizontal position all four limbs would be needed for support."

"Yes, but why should four be the limit?"

"Men with six arms?"

"Perhaps. On planets where the force of gravity is very great the vertebrates would most likely develop precisely in that direction. But there are other factors. The condition of the planet's surface, for instance. If the Earth had been permanently covered with oceans the evolution of the animal world would have taken an entirely different course."

"Mermaids?" I jokingly suggested.

"Possibly," Nikonov replied imperturbably. "Life in the ocean is constantly developing although much more slowly than on dry land. There are certain things essential to all rational beings, wherever they happen to live: a developed brain, a complex nervous system, and organs enabling them to work and move. But this is hardly enough to give one any real idea of their general appearance."

"But surely," I persisted, unwilling to yield, "it is not altogether unlikely that thinking beings resembling ourselves may live on planets with conditions similar to our own, is it?"

"It is not impossible," he agreed. "But highly improbable. You disregard one very important factor—time. Man's appearance changes. Ten million years ago our ancestors had tails and no foreheads. How do we know what men will look like ten million years hence? It would be absurd to assume that man's appearance will never change. You talk about similar planets. True, there are planets with conditions similar to our own. But it is hardly likely that the evolution of rational beings on these planets would coincide in time as well. In a word, my dear friend, 'There are more things on heaven and earth....' "

I cannot remember all the details of that conversation. There were so many interruptions—the telephone rang constantly, people hurried in and out of the room and Nikonov kept consulting his watch. Yet looking back at it now it seems to me that that conversation was in itself significant. For fantastic as our surmises might have seemed, the reality exceeded our wildest speculations.

It all seems simple enough to me now. If a ship from another planetary system reached us through boundless space, knowledge on that unknown planet had clearly advanced to a degree far beyond our earthly conception. That alone should have warned us not to jump to conclusions.

The arrival of Academician Astakhov, a specialist in astronautical medicine, cut short our conversation.

"What sort of an engine has it?" he demanded from the threshold.

He stood in the doorway, his ear cupped in his hand, waiting for an answer.

I felt annoyed with myself for not having asked that obvious question. The answer would have told us many things—the technical level of the newcomers, the distance they had flown, how much time they had journeyed in space, what rates of acceleration their bodies could endure....

"There is no engine," said Nikonov. "The metallic cylinder underneath the stone envelope is absolutely smooth."

"No engine?" echoed Astakhov. He pondered this in silence for a few minutes, a look of profound amazement on his face. "But in that case.... In that case they must have a gravitational engine."

"Yes," nodded Nikonov. "That's the answer, most likely."

"Can you power a ship by gravitation?" I asked.

"Theoretically you can," Nikonov replied

"There is no natural force which man will not eventually be able to understand and subdue. It is only a matter of time. True, so far we know very little about gravitation. We know Newton's law: every body in the Universe attracts every other body with a force that is directly proportional to the product of their masses, and inversely proportional to the square of the distance between their centres. We know, theoretically at least, that the only limit to gravitational acceleration is the speed of light. But that is about all. But the cause, the nature of gravitation—that we don't know."

The phone rang again. Nikonov picked up the receiver, answered briefly and hung up.

"Come," he said to us. "They are waiting for us."

We went out into the corridor.

"Some physicists believe that gravitation is a property of a specific type of particles called gravitons. I am not quite sure of that hypothesis. But if it is true, then the gravitons ought to be as much smaller than atomic nuclei as the atomic nuclei are smaller than ordinary bodies. The concentration of energy must be immeasurably greater in such minute dimensions than in the atomic nucleus."

We hurried down the steep winding staircase

leading to the basement and along a narrow corridor. A group of institute personnel were waiting for us outside a massive metal door. Someone pressed a button and the door moved slowly aside.

There was the space ship: a cylinder of some dark and very smooth metal, resting on two supports. The stone outer covering, cracked in several places, had been removed. Three fine wires hung from the base of the cylinder.

Nikonov who stood closer than the others to the cylinder took a step toward it and at once a muffled knocking sounded from within. It was not the rhythmic mechanical beat of a machine. It suggested the presence of some living creature. It occurred to me that it might be some animal—after all, had we not sent monkeys, dogs and rabbits up in our own space rockets?

Nikonov moved away and the knocking ceased. In the ensuing silence someone's hoarse breathing could be distinctly heard.

Strangely enough, no thought of the new epoch that had dawned for science entered my mind at that moment. It was only afterwards in recalling the scene that I found every detail of it stamped on my memory: the low-ceilinged room flooded with electric light, and in the middle—the dark, gleaming cylinder, and the tense, excited faces of the men gathered around it.

We set to work at once. It was the engineers' task to determine what was inside the cylinder; Astakhov's and mine, to provide two-way biological protection—to protect the living creatures within from our earthly bacteria, and ourselves from any bacteria the space ship might contain.

I do not know exactly how the engineers tackled their part of the job. I had no time to see what they were doing. I only remember that they subjected the cylinder to ultra-sound and gamma radiation. Astakhov and I went to work on the biological end. After some discussion (Astakhov's being hard of hearing delayed things somewhat), it was decided to open the cylinder with manipulators operated from the distance. The sealed chamber in which the space ship stood was to be treated with ultra-violet rays.

We worked at top speed, conscious of the living creature near by awaiting our assistance. We did everything that was humanly possible to do.

The manipulators using a hydrogen burner carefully cut through the metal covering in which the space ship's apparatus was encased. Through slit-windows in the concrete wall of the room we watched the remarkable accuracy and precision with which the huge mechanical hands worked. Slowly, centimetre by centimetre, the flame of the burner cut through the strange, highly refractory metal, until at last the base of the cylinder could be removed.

What lay inside was living matter if not a living creature—a giant brain throbbing with life.

I use the word "brain" solely for want of any other word to describe what I saw. For a moment it looked to me like an exact replica, if magnified, of the human brain. On closer examination however I saw where I had been mistaken. It was only part of a brain. What was missing, we discovered later, were all those departments, all those centres that govern the emotions and instincts. Moreover, it had only a few of the innumerable "thinking" centres of the human brain, though these were enormously magnified.

To be more exact, it was a neutron computing machine with artificial brain matter in place of the usual electronic diodes and triodes. I surmised this at once from a great number of minor indications, but my supposition later proved to be correct.

Somewhere, on some unknown planet, science had advanced far beyond our own. We on Earth have only begun to synthesize the simplest protein molecules. *They* had succeeded in synthesizing the highest forms of organic matter. We biochemists too are working toward that end, but we are still very far from our goal.

I must admit that the contents of the space ship were a great surprise to all of us. All except Astakhov. He was the first to recover the power of speech.

"There you are!" he exclaimed. "Exactly what I predicted! You may remember what I wrote two years ago.... Inter-stellar distances are too great for man. Only space ships that operate completely automatically can undertake journeys from one island universe to another. Automatically! Electronic machines, perhaps? No, too complicated. Out of the question. What is needed is the most perfect of all mechanisms—the brain. Two years ago I wrote about this. But some biochemists did not agree with me. I said that for interstellar travel we must have bio-automatons, capable of cellular regeneration...."

Astakhov had indeed published an article two years before advancing this idea. I confess it had sounded utterly fantastic to me. Yet he had been right after all. He had foreseen the possibility of synthesizing the highest form of matter—brain tissue—thus anticipating scientific progress by many centuries.

It must be admitted that we scientists who work in narrow fields show little imagination in predicting the future. We are far too engrossed in what we are doing in the present to foresee the shape of things to come. There are automobiles today, and in a hundred years there will be automobiles too, only with far greater speeds. Similarly we cannot imagine that the airplane of the future will differ greatly from the present except in the matter of speed. But, alas, that only shows how limited our vision is. And that is why the shape of the Future is often more clearly envisioned by non-specialists.

Sometimes that Future seems altogether incredible, altogether fantastic and unattainable. Nevertheless it comes to pass! Heinrich Hertz, who was the first to study electromagnetic vibrations, rejected the idea of wireless communication. Yet a few years later Alexander Popov invented the radio.

Yes, I had not believed in Astakhov's idea. In order to produce bio-automatons some extremely complex problems would have to be solved. We would have to synthesize the highest forms of proteins, learn to control bio-electronic processes, induce living and non-living matter to work together. All this seemed to me to belong to the realm of sheer fantasy. Yet here right before our eyes was that distant Future. True, it was the fruit of the endeavours of men from another planet than ours, but nonetheless tangible confirmation of the great truth that there can be no limits to scientific knowledge, no idea too bold to be realized.

We did not know anything about the atmosphere inside the cylinder and how our own atmosphere would affect the artificial brain. Therefore compressor units and gas containers were held in readiness to adjust the atmosphere inside the sealed chamber to that in the cylinder. When the cylinder was opened the atmosphere inside it was found to consist of one-fifth oxygen and four-fifth helium at a pressure one-tenth greater than that on Earth. The brain continued to pulsate, though perhaps a little faster than before.

There was a whining sound as the compressors went into action to raise the pressure. The first stage of the work was over.

I went upstairs to Nikonov's office. I moved his armchair over to the window and raised the blinds. Outside dusk was settling over the city. Night had come again, the second night since I had been summoned to the institute. Yet it seemed I had been there only a few hours.

So the atmosphere in the space ship was 20 per cent oxygen—the same as in the Earth's atmosphere. Was this fortuitous? No. This was exactly the concentration the human organism needs. Hence, there must be some sort of circulatory system in the space ship. But if one part of the brain should die, circulation would be disrupted and hence the entire brain would perish.

This thought sent me hurrying downstairs again.

Even as I recall our efforts to save the artificial brain I am overwhelmed again by a feeling of impotence and bitterness.

What could we do? Nothing. Nothing but look on helplessly while the brain that had come to us from outer space, the brain created by the inhabitants of another planet, slowly expired.

The lower part dried up and turned black. Only the upper section remained throbbingly alive. When anyone approached it the throbbing became quick and feverish, as if the brain were calling frantically for help.

By now we knew how the brain was supplied with oxygen. As 1 had presumed, it breathed with the help of a chemical compound resembling haemoglobin. We had also studied the devices that fed the brain, generated oxygen and removed the carbon dioxide from the atmosphere.

Yet we could do nothing to halt the destruction of the brain cells. Somewhere, on an unknown planet, thinking beings had been able to synthesize the most highly organized matter—brain matter. They had created an artificial brain and sent it out into space. There was no doubt that many of the secrets of the Universe were recorded in those brain cells. But we could not fathom them. The brain was dying before our eyes.

We tried everything, from antibiotics to surgery. Nothing helped.

In my capacity as chairman of the Special Commission of the Academy of Sciences I called a conference of my colleagues to ascertain whether there was anything else that could be done.

It was in the early hours before dawn. The scientists sat in the small conference hall in gloomy silence, their faces drawn with fatigue.

Nikonov passed a hand over his face as if to brush away his weariness.

"There is nothing more to be done," he said in a flat voice.

The others confirmed this tragic fact.

Throughout the next six days, while the few remaining cells of the artificial brain still lived, we kept up constant observations. It is hard to enumerate all that we learned in that time. But the most interesting was the discovery of the substance that protected the living tissue from radiation.

The outer shell of the space ship was comparatively thin and could be easily penetrated by cosmic rays. This had prompted us from the very outset to search for some protective substance in the cells of the bio-automaton itself. And we found it. A minute concentration of this substance immunizes the body against the most powerful radiation. This discovery will enable us to simplify the design of our own space ships. It obviates the need for heavy metal shields for the atomic reactor, and this brings the era of space travel in atom-powered ships much closer.

Extremely interesting too was the system for regeneration of oxygen. A colony of seaweed unknown to us and weighing less than a kilogram which absorbed carbon dioxide and exhaled oxygen had provided the ship with adequate "air conditioning" for many years.

But all these are purely biological discoveries. The knowledge gained in the sphere of engineering is perhaps even more important. As Astakhov had surmised, the space ship was powered by a gravitation engine. Engineers have not yet grasped the principle of the mechanism. But it may be safely asserted that our physicists will have substantially to revise their ideas about the nature of gravitation. The epoch of atomic engineering will evidently be followed by an epoch of gravitational engineering, when men will have still greater sources of energy and speed at their disposal.

The outer covering of the space ship consisted of an alloy of titanium and beryllium. As distinct from the usual alloys, the entire casing was made of a single-crystal metal. Our metals consist, roughly speaking, of myriads of crystals. And although each of them is strong enough, they do not cohere too well. The future belongs to the single-crystal metal, which will have properties we still have to discover. Moreover, by governing the systems of crystallization, man will be able to govern its optical properties, durability and heat conductivity at will.

Nevertheless the most important discovery of all, though not as yet deciphered, is connected with the artificial brain. The three wires attached to the cylinder proved to be connected with the brain through a rather complicated amplifying system. For six days sensitive oscillographs registered the bio-automaton's currents. These currents were nothing like those of the human brain. And this is where the difference between the artificial and the human brain was manifested. After all, the brain of the space ship was essentially nothing more than a cybernetic device, with living cells taking the place of electronic tubes. With all its complex structure this brain was immeasurably simpler and, as it were, more specialized than the human brain. Hence its electrical signals resembled a code more than the extremely complex pattern of biocurrents in the human brain.

Thousands of metres of oscillograms were recorded in those six days. Will it be possible to decipher them? What will they tell us? The story of a voyage through space perhaps?

It is hard to answer these questions. We are continuing to study the space ship and each day brings some new discovery.

So far many know much about this stone, everyone knows something, but nobody knows enough. But the day is not far off when the last secrets of the star stone will be fathomed.

And then space ships powered with gravitational engines will set out from the Earth for the boundless expanses of the Universe. They will be manned not by human beings—for man's life is brief, and the Universe is infinite. The interstellar ships will be manned by bio-automatons. After voyaging thousands of years in space, after reaching distant island universes, the ships will come back to Earth bearing the unfading torch of Knowledge.

> V. Zhuravleva's story "Stone From the Stars" treats of bio-automatons. The problem posed is "to synthesize the highest forms of biological matter, learn to control electronic

processes and induce living and non-living matter to work together. The story is about a bio-automaton serving as the "brain" of a space ship in which "living cells take the place of electronic tubes."

That living matter may be produced synthetically is recognized by our philosophy. The subject of Zhuravleva's story rests on hypothesis as well as scientific fact. Scientists are already working on the idea of incorporating bio-energetic elements in machines. It is to the author's credit that she seeks to popularize this idea. True, the story contains some highly questionable theories, such as those concerning regeneration of brain cells. Attractive though this idea may be, it has so far not found sufficient confirmation.

> A. A. *Malinovsky*, M. Sc. (Biol.)
> S. A. *Stebakov*, member, Bureau of the mathematical Biology Section, Moscow Naturalists' Society

ARKADY AND BORIS STRUGATSKY

SIX MATCHES

I

The Inspector laid aside his notebook.

"This is a very strange business, Comrade Leman. Very strange indeed."

"Do you think so?" said the Director of the institute.

"Don't you?"

"No, I don't. I think everything is perfectly clear."

The Director spoke drily, staring out of the window at the empty sun-flooded square. His neck had been aching for some time, and there was nothing of any interest on the square, yet he stubbornly kept his face averted. It was a kind of mute protest. The Director was young and inclined to be touchy. He knew quite well what the Inspector meant, but he did not think the Inspector had any right to harp on that particular aspect of the affair. The man's quiet insistence irritated him. "Why can't he leave well enough alone?" he thought in annoyance. "It's all as clear as daylight."

"It's not all clear to me," said the Inspector.

The Director shrugged his shoulders. He glanced at his watch and rose.

"Excuse me, Comrade Rybnikov," he said. "I have a class in five minutes. I'd better be going if you don't need me."

"Go ahead, Comrade Leman. I should like to see that, er ... that 'personal laboratory assistant.' Gorchinsky is the name, I believe?"

"Yes, Gorchinsky. He hasn't come back yet. He will be told to see you as soon as he comes."

The Director nodded and withdrew. The Inspector looked after him with a quizzical expression on his face. "A little too cocksure, my friend," he said to himself. "Never mind. I'll get around to you eventually."

But the Director's turn hadn't come yet. There were more important things to be attended to first. On the face of it everything really did seem to be quite clear. Inspector Rybnikov of the Labour Protection Board could have written up his report on the "Case of Andrei Andreyevich Komlin, chief of the physics laboratory of the Central Brain Institute" without further delay. Andrei Komlin had performed some dangerous experiments on himself and had been rushed to hospital three days before where he still lay in a semi-delirious condition, his shaven head covered with some mysterious ringed bruises. He had lost the power of speech, was being treated with diverse stimulants and all that the doctors could say at this stage was that it was a case of extreme nervous exhaustion, which had affected the memory, speech and hearing centres.

As far as the Labour Protection Board was concerned this was an open-and-shut case. It was not a matter of machines or apparatus being out of order, or of carelessness or incompetence on anyone's part. There had been no violation of safety rules, at least not in the generally accepted sense. It was obvious too that Komlin had performed the experiments on himself in secret, and that no one at the institute had known anything about it, not even Alexander Gorchinsky, his "personal" laboratory assistant—although some of the other laboratory workers were of a different opinion on that score.

The Inspector was interested in another angle of the affair. A former research worker himself, Rybnikov sensed that behind the odd bits of information he had elicited concerning Komlin's work and this mysterious accident of his there lay some extraordinary scientific discovery. And the more he thought about it the more convinced he became that this was so.

Three months before the accident the laboratory had received a new apparatus: a neutrino beam generator. It was the advent of the generator in the physics laboratory that had set off the chain of events which, owing to what the Inspector considered downright negligence on the part of those concerned, had finally led to disaster.

Soon after the arrival of the generator, Komlin had turned over all his current work to his deputy and had shut himself up in the room where the new apparatus stood, announcing his intention to prepare a series of preliminary experiments. This went on for several days, at the end of which time Komlin reappeared, made his usual round of the laboratory, gave three staff members a dressing-down, signed some papers and ordered his deputy to get busy with the semi-annual report. The following day he locked himself up with the generator again, this time taking Alexander Gorchinsky with him.

What they did there came to light only two days before the accident, when Komlin had delivered a sensational report on neutrino acupuncture that had "shaken the foundations of medical science." But in the course of his three months' work with the generator Komlin had attracted the attention of his institute colleagues on three different occasions.

The first was when he turned up one fine day with his hair shaved off and a small black skull cap perched on his bald pate. That fact alone might have passed unnoticed had it not been for the peculiar behaviour of Gorchinsky that same morning. An hour after he and his chief had locked themselves in their laboratory, he came dashing out of the room, pale and dishevelled and rushed over wildly to the laboratory medicine chest. With trembling fingers he seized a few first-aid kits and dashed back to the generator chamber slamming the door behind him. Before the door closed, however, someone had caught a glimpse of Komlin by the window, clutching his left hand which was smeared with something that looked like blood. That evening Komlin and Gorchinsky had slipped quietly out of the neutrino chamber and hurried out of the laboratory without a word to anyone. Both seemed extremely depressed, and Komlin's left hand was bound in a soiled bandage.

The next curious thing happened a month later. One evening a junior member of the staff named Vedeneyev met Komlin in a secluded corner of the Blue Park. Komlin was seated on a park bench with a thick and dog-eared volume on his knees, staring before him and muttering under his breath. Vedeneyev wished him a good evening and sat down beside him. Komlin ceased his mutterings at once and turned to him, his neck sticking out strangely. His eyes, according to Vedeneyev, had what he described as a "murky look" and the young man had a strong desire to get up and go at once. But since that did not seem the polite thing to do, he tried to make conversation.

"Reading, Andrei Andreyevich?" he inquired.

"Yes," said Komlin. "Shih Nai-ang, *River Backwaters*. Most interesting. Take this, for instance...."

Vedeneyev was too young to know much about the Chinese classics and he felt even more uncomfortable than before. But Komlin suddenly closed the book with a bang, handed it to Vedeneyev and asked him to open it at random. Slightly embarrassed, Vedeneyev obeyed. Komlin glanced at the page ("once, and only for a moment"), and nodded.

"Now follow the text," he said.

And in his clear, distinct voice he proceeded to tell how one Hu Yang-cho, brandishing his sabre pounced on Ho Cheng and Se Pao, and how the "short-clawed tiger" Wang Ying and his wife "The Green Lady".... At that point Vedeneyev realized that Komlin was reciting the text from memory. He did not miss a single line, he did not stumble over a single name. He recited the entire page, word for word, letter for letter. When he came to the end, he asked:

"Any mistakes?"

Speechless with amazement, Vedeneyev shook his head. Komlin laughed, picked up the book and walked off. Vedeneyev did not know what to think. When he related the incident to his comrades they advised him to ask Komlin himself for an explanation. But when Vedeneyev made some remark to Komlin about that meeting in the park, the latter seemed so genuinely amazed and puzzled that Vedeneyev dropped the subject.

But even more odd was what had happened a few hours before the fatal accident.

That evening Komlin, sparkling with gaiety and good humour, demonstrated some conjuring tricks to his colleagues. He had an audience of four—Alexander Gorchinsky, his adoring, unshaven assistant, and the three young girl assistants, Lena, Dusya and Katya, who had stayed behind to finish up some urgent work.

The tricks were quite sensational. To begin with Komlin offered to hypnotize someone, and when no one agreed, he told a funny story about a hypnotist and a surgeon.

"Now then, Lena," he said. "Would you like me to guess what you have hidden in the drawer of your desk?"

Two of his three guesses were correct. Dusya accused him of peeping. He denied the charge, but the girls continued to tease him, whereupon he announced that he could extinguish a flame merely by looking at it. Dusya snatched up a box of matches, ran off into a corner of the room, and struck a match. It flared up and went out at once. Everyone was amazed and all eyes were turned to Komlin. He stood with his arms folded over his chest, his brows knitted in the classical pose of the professional conjuror.

"What powerful lungs!" said Dusya admiringly. Komlin was standing a good ten paces away from her. Komlin then told them to tie a handkerchief over his mouth. When this was done, Dusya struck another match, and again it went out.

"Do you blow through your nose then?" said the amazed Dusya. Komlin tore off the handkerchief, burst out laughing and seizing Dusya waltzed around the room with her.

After that he performed two more tricks: he dropped a match and instead of falling straight down it fell sideways at a considerable angle. ("You're blowing at it again," Dusya said uncertainly.) Then he laid a piece of tungsten spiral on the table and the spiral crawled over the glass top to the edge of the desk and fell on the floor. Everyone was astonished, of course, and Gorchinsky begged him to tell them how it was done. But Komlin suddenly turned serious and offered to multiply several sums in his head.

"Six hundred and fifty-four by two hundred and thirty-one and the result by sixteen," Katya said timidly.

"Take a pencil and write," Komlin ordered in a strained voice and proceeded to dictate: "Four, eight, one ..." his voice dropped to a whisper, and he wound up in one breath: "Seven, one, four, two.... Right to left."

He turned (the girls were shocked at the change in him—his whole figure seemed suddenly to droop) and shuffled heavily over to the generator chamber and locked himself in again. Gorchinsky, who had been checking the figures, stared after him anxiously for a few moments and then announced that the answer was correct—reading the figures from right to left the answer was two million four hundred and seventeen thousand one hundred and eighty-four.

The girls worked until ten o'clock that evening. Gorchinsky also stayed behind, but he was too restless to be of much help to them. Komlin did not reappear. At ten they said good night to him through the door and went home. The next morning Komlin was taken to hospital.

The "official" result of Komlin's three months' research was "neutrino acupuncture," a method of treatment by directing streams of neutrinos at the brain. The new method was tremendously interesting in itself, but what was the explanation for Komlin's injured hand? Or his phenomenal memory? And what about the tricks with the matches, the spirals and his lightning calculation?

"He kept it all a secret from his colleagues,"

the Inspector murmured. "I wonder why? Was it because he was unsure of himself or because he did not want to endanger his comrades? Odd. Very odd indeed."

The videophone clicked and the face of his secretary appeared on the screen.

"Comrade Gorchinsky is here," she said.

"Show him in," said the Inspector.

II

A burly giant of a man in a checked shirt with rolled-up sleeves appeared in the doorway. The Inspector got the impression of a powerful neck, massive shoulders, and a large head covered with a shock of thick black hair, with, surprisingly, a small bald spot (two small bald spots, in fact) in the middle, for the man came into the room backwards. He was holding the door open for someone else who turned out to be the Director. The man in the checked shirt closed the door after him, then turned and made a curt bow. He wore a small but very bushy moustache and his expression was rather grim. This was Alexander Gorchinsky, Komlin's "personal" laboratory assistant.

The Director sank into an armchair and stared out of the window. Gorchinsky stood before the Inspector in an expectant attitude.

"Will you ..." the Inspector began.

"Thanks, I will," boomed the laboratory assistant and sat down, placing his hands on his knees and turning a pair of steely grey eyes on the Inspector.

"Gorchinsky, I presume?" asked the Inspector.

"That's right. Alexander Borisovich Gorchinsky."

"Pleased to meet you. My name is Rybnikov, I am the Labour Protection Inspector."

"This is a pleasure, Inspector," drawled Gorchinsky with exaggerated politeness.

"You are Komlin's 'personal' laboratory assistant."

"I don't know what you mean by 'personal'. I'm a member of the staff of the physics laboratory of the Central Brain Institute."

The Inspector glanced quickly at the Director and caught a faint ironical twinkle in his eye.

"Do you mind telling me exactly what problems you have been working on during the past three months?"

"We have been doing some research in neutrino acupuncture."

"Could you be a little more explicit, please?"

"There is a detailed report on the subject," said Gorchinsky stiffly. "You will find everything there."

"No doubt. Nevertheless I would be much obliged if you would clarify the term for me," said the Inspector very calmly.

For a few seconds the two men looked each other squarely in the eye, the Inspector's face slowly reddening, Gorchinsky's moustache bristling. At length the laboratory assistant narrowed his eyes.

"Very well," he boomed. "If you insist. We were studying the action of focussed neutrino beams on the grey and white matter of the brain, and on the animal organism in general...."

He spoke in a flat toneless voice, and seemed to be swaying slightly as he spoke.

"... Besides registering pathological and other changes in the organism, we measured the activated currents, differential decrement and lability curves in various tissues, as well as the relative quantities of neuroglobulin and neurostromin...."

The Inspector leaned back in his chair, listening with mixed admiration and annoyance. "You just wait, my fine fellow!" he thought. The Director continued to stare out of the window, drumming his fingers on the table.

"Tell me, Comrade Gorchinsky, what has happened to your hands?" the Inspector asked, cutting the laboratory assistant short. The Inspector disliked being put on the defensive. He preferred to take the initiative.

Gorchinsky glanced down at his hands lying on the arms of the chair. They were a mass of scratches and dark blue scars. He made an involuntary movement as if to thrust them into his pockets, but instead he slowly clenched his huge fists.

"The monkey we were experimenting with scratched me up," he muttered.

"Did you experiment on animals only?"

"Yes. I experimented only on animals," said Gorchinsky, faintly emphasizing the "I."

"What sort of an accident did Komlin have two months ago?" the Inspector asked quickly.

Gorchinsky shrugged his shoulders.

"I don't remember."

"Let me refresh your memory. Komlin cut his hand. How did it happen?"

"How should I know? He just cut himself and that's all I know."

"Alexander Borisovich!" the Director said reprovingly.

"Why don't you ask Komlin himself?" Gorchinsky said defiantly.

The Inspector's eyes narrowed.

"You astound me, Gorchinsky," he said softly. "You seem to think I'm trying to pump you for information that might compromise Komlin ... or yourself, or your colleagues. But it is all far simpler than that. You see, I am not a specialist in the central nervous system. Radio-optics is my line. That's all. What's more, I have no right to judge by my own personal impressions. I am not here to weave elaborate theories. I am here to discover the truth. And instead of helping me you behave like a hysterical woman. You ought to be ashamed of yourself."

There was a silence. The Director looked at Rybnikov. He began to understand the secret of this man's power. Gorchinsky evidently felt it too, because finally he blurted out, avoiding everyone's eyes:

"What is it you want to know?"

"I want to know more about this neutrino acupuncture, for one thing."

"It is Andrei Andreyevich's idea," Gorchinsky began in a weary voice. "Bombardment of certain regions of the cortex with streams of neutrinos induces resistance to various chemical poisons or toxins, or, to be more exact, sharply increases it. Infected or poisoned dogs recovered completely after two or three neutrino punctures, as we call it by analogy with the old method of inserting needles into the tissue. You see, the role of the needles is played by neutrino beams. Of course the analogy is purely superficial...."

"How is it done practically?" asked the Inspector.

"The scalp is shaved and compact devices for focussing the neutrino beams are attached to the bare skin by means of suction discs. To aim the beam at the required stratum of grey matter is not easy, but to locate the exact regions of the cortex that would stimulate phagocyte activity in the required direction is even harder."

"That is very interesting indeed," said the Inspector and this time he meant it. "What diseases could be cured by this method?"

Gorchinsky was silent for a few moments.

"A great many," he said finally. "Andrei Andreyevich believes that neutrino acupuncture has the effect of mobilizing, as it were, some unknown forces of the organism. Not only phagocytes, or nervous stimuli, but something far more powerful. But he did not complete his research.... He said neutrino bombardment would be able to cure any disease—toxic poisoning, heart disease, malignant tumours...."

"Cancer?"

"Yes. And burns.... It might even be able to restore dead organs. He said that the stabilizing forces of the human body are tremendous, and that the key to them is in the cortex. One has only to find the exact points in the cortex for the punctures."

"Neutrino acupuncture," the Inspector said slowly, savouring the peculiar flavour of the words. Then he caught himself. "Very good, Comrade Gorchinsky. I am much obliged to you." (Gorchinsky smiled ruefully.) "And now be so kind as to tell us how you found Komlin on the morning of the accident. I gather you were the first to see him?"

"Yes. When I came to work I found him sitting, or rather lying in his armchair at the desk...."

"In the generator room?"

"Yes. The focussing devices were attached to his skull with suction discs and the generator was switched on. I thought at first that he was dead. I ran for the doctor. That's all."

His voice shook. The Inspector looked up quickly in surprise. He paused for a moment before asking the next question. The Director drummed loudly on the desk, staring into space.

"You say you don't know what Komlin's experiment was?"

"No," replied the laboratory assistant hoarsely. "I don't know. The laboratory scales and two boxes of matches stood on the table in front of him. The matches had fallen out of one of the boxes."

"One moment." The Inspector glanced at the Director and turned back to Gorchinsky.

"Matches, you say? What could he have been doing with matches?"

"I don't know," said Gorchinsky. "There was a heap of them. Some were glued together in twos and threes. There were six matches lying on the scales. And a sheet of paper with figures. He had been weighing the matches. I know, because I checked the figures."

"Matches," murmured the Inspector. "Now why matches? Any idea, Comrade Gorchinsky?"

"No."

"Your colleagues mentioned something about matches too," said the Inspector, rubbing his chin thoughtfully. "Those tricks he performed ... with fire ... and matches.... Evidently he was working on some other problems besides neutrino acupuncture. But what?"

Gorchinsky said nothing.

"He frequently experimented on himself, didn't he? The skin on his skull is covered with the marks of those suction discs you spoke of."

Gorchinsky remained silent.

"Had Komlin ever displayed an ability to make rapid calculations in his head? Before he demonstrated those conjuring tricks, I mean?"

"No," said Gorchinsky. "I hadn't noticed anything of that kind. Well, now you know all that I know myself. Yes, it is true that Andrei

Andreyevich experimented with neutrino bombardment on himself. He cut his hand with a razor deliberately. He wanted to see how quickly neutrino acupuncture could heal wounds. It didn't work ... that time. He was doing a parallel piece of research which he kept a secret from everyone. Myself included. I do not know what it was. I only know it had also something to do with neutrino radiation. And that's all."

"Did anyone know of this besides yourself?" the Inspector asked.

"No. Not a soul."

"And you know nothing about the experiments Komlin performed without your assistance?"

"Nothing."

"Well, that will be all," said the Inspector. "You may go."

Gorchinsky rose and strode to the door without looking up. Watching him go, the Inspector noticed again the bald spots on his scalp.

The Director stared out of the window. A small helicopter was hovering low over the square. Its silvery body gleamed in the sunlight as, swaying gently, it turned slowly around its axis and touched down. The door opened and the pilot in a suit of grey overalls jumped lightly on the pavement and walked briskly toward the institute, lighting a cigarette as he went. The Director recognized the helicopter. It was the Inspector's. The pilot had evidently been refuelling.

"Is there no danger of neutrino acupuncture affecting the mind?" the Inspector asked.

"No," replied the Director. "Komlin was quite emphatic on that point."

The Inspector leaned back in his chair and gazed at the ceiling.

"You shouldn't have been so hard on Gorchinsky. He won't be able to do a stroke of work today," said the Director in a low tone.

"Nonsense," said the Inspector. "I'm surprised at you, Comrade Leman. Tell me, how many bald spots is it normal for a man to have? And all those scars on his hands.... If you ask me, Komlin has an extremely apt pupil in Gorchinsky."

"These men are passionately devoted to their work," said the Director.

The Inspector regarded him for a few minutes without speaking, his facial muscles working.

"I do not doubt that," he said. "Nevertheless, they still work in the old way, Comrade Leman. And, unfortunately, you encourage them. Look here, we are a rich country, the richest in the world. We give you scientists any amount of apparatus, all the experimental animals you want and everything else you need for your work. Then why do you permit your people to take such risks? You have no right to be so careless about human life."

"I...."

"Why are you not fulfilling the April Directives of the Central Committee? Why are you not carrying out the decision of the Presidium of the Supreme Soviet? When will these scandalous practices stop?"

"This is the first time anything like this has happened at our institute," the Director said resentfully.

The Inspector shook his head.

"At your institute, perhaps. But what about other institutes? What about the factories? This is the eighth accident in the past six months. It's barbarous! Barbarous heroism! You can't keep them out of automatic rockets, out of autobathyspheres or reactors...." He laughed drily. "They are trying to take a short cut to the Truth, to victory over Nature. But too often they pay with their lives. And now your Komlin has done the same thing. How could you have allowed it, Professor?"

The Director frowned.

"Sometimes it is inevitable," he said. "Have you forgotten all those doctors who used to inject themselves with cholera and plague germs?"

"Why must we go so far back? After all, that is ancient history by now!"

They lapsed into silence. Day was drawing to a close and grey shadows gathered in the corners of the room.

"Incidentally," the Director said, avoiding the Inspector's eye, "I ordered Komlin's safe to be broken open, and I have his notebooks. They might interest you."

"Most certainly," said the Inspector.

"Only I'm afraid you won't learn very much from them," the Director said with an apologetic smile. "It's all very specialized stuff. If you like I can take them home with me this evening and try to compile a digest for you...."

The Inspector was frankly relieved at the suggestion.

"But you mustn't expect too much," the Director hastened to add. "These neutrino beams.... You know, it was like a bolt from the blue for all of us. No one had ever imagined anything like it. Komlin is a pioneer in this field, the first in the world. So I'm not sure I'll be able to make much of his notes either."

The Inspector sat for a while after the Director had gone, thinking over what he had heard. He fervently hoped that Komlin's notes would shed some light on the affair. He pictured Komlin seated at his desk with a set of electrodes on his shaven head, weighing matches glued together.

No, acupuncture had nothing to do with it. This was something altogether new, something Komlin himself scarcely believed in, judging by the care he had taken to hide his gruesome experiments from his colleagues.

Yes, this was a wonderful age, the Inspector thought. Wonderful people too, these Communists of the fourth generation. Like their predecessors, they forged boldly ahead with little thought of themselves, from year to year advancing more and more daringly into the unknown. It required tremendous efforts to channel this vast ocean of enthusiasm so as to use it with maximum effect. Mankind's victory over Nature must be won through the medium of ingenious machines and devices and precision instruments, not by sacrificing the lives of its finest representatives. And not only because those who live today can accomplish far more than those who died yesterday, but also because Man is the most precious thing on Earth.

The Inspector rose heavily from his chair and limped over to the door. He moved slowly and painfully for three reasons—in the first place by habit, secondly, he was beginning to feel his age, and thirdly, his leg bothered him.

"Those old wounds of mine," he muttered as he limped down the corridor.

III

Early next morning, at the very hour when the doctors, having failed to diagnose Komlin's complaint, noted with relief that the patient was regaining his power of speech, Rybnikov and Leman were sitting in the Director's office, facing each other again across the huge desk.

The Inspector had a thick notebook on his knees, while the Director was looking through a heap of papers—notes, diagrams, drawings and sketches.

The Director spoke rapidly, at times disjointedly. His eyes, red-rimmed from lack of sleep, looked through the Inspector. Now and again he would stop in the middle of a phrase as if astounded at the import of his own words. The Inspector listened intently, and gradually out of the vast mass of incredible facts and data a general pattern began to emerge. Here is what he learned.

Komlin was keenly interested in the effect of neutrino beams on brain tissue, firstly because literally nothing was known about it. It was only recently that streams of neutrinos of an intensity great enough to be of practical value had been obtained, and as soon as the neutrino generator arrived Komlin decided to see what could be done with it.

Secondly, Komlin expected a great deal from these experiments. High-energy radiation (nucleons, electrons, gamma rays) disrupted the molecular and intra-atomic structure of the proteins of the brain, in other words, destroyed the brain. It could produce nothing but pathological changes in the organism—this had been proved experimentally. The neutrino—that infinitesimally small neutral particle with no rest mass—was quite a different matter. Komlin assumed that it would produce no explosive reaction or changes in molecular structure, but would merely cause moderate excitation in the brain protein, strengthening the nuclear fields and perhaps creating new, hitherto unknown fields of force. All of Komlin's hypotheses proved to be correct.

"Much of what was in the notebooks is unintelligible to me," the Director interrupted himself to remark. "Some things I simply refuse to believe. That is why I am only giving you a very rough sketch in the hope that it will shed some light on the mystery of those conjuring tricks. Although that too is fantastic enough."

The idea for neutrino acupuncture struck Komlin as soon as he began experimenting on animals. The monkey he was working with injured its paw, and the wound healed with amazing speed. So did the dark spots in the animal's lungs, traces of tuberculosis so common in monkeys living in moderate climates.

The work on neutrino acupuncture proceeded successfully. Several dogs injected with diverse biological poisons were rapidly cured by the neutrino treatment. Komlin's needle (as Gorchinsky named the method) cured tuberculosis in monkeys dozens of times faster and more successfully than the most effective antibiotics.

At this stage there was no actual need for experimenting on human beings; Komlin was not yet working on the method of treatment, he was only proving its feasibility in principle. In his famous report he had voiced the assumption that the human and animal organism possessed some hidden curative powers which were so far unknown to science, but which had already manifested themselves during the experiments with neutrino acupuncture. He had worked out a detailed program for switching over from experiments on animals to experiments on human beings—a carefully thought-out fool-proof scheme, providing for a wide margin of error and for the gradual advance from the simplest and obviously harmless neutrino punctures to more complicated, combined ones. The program provided for the participation in the work of large groups of doctors, physiologists and psychologists. But....

The Inspector had not been mistaken. Komlin had not only been working on neutrino acupuncture. Before long the experiments with the neutrino generator showed that the extraordinary development of the curative powers of the organism, though important, was by no means the only effect of neutrino beams on the brain. The experimental animals behaved very strangely. True, not all of them and not always. It was observed that most of those that had been given brief treatments behaved normally, but the "favourites," those that had been subjected to numerous and diverse experiments, gave the two researchers some surprises. But while the young laboratory assistant Gorchinsky regarded their antics as amusing or annoying tricks of Nature, Komlin with his scientific intuition sensed that they were on the track of an important scientific discovery.

The dog Genny (short for "Generator") showed a sudden talent for circus tricks though no one had taught him; he would "shake hands," walk on his hind legs and even on his forepaws, and one day Gorchinsky had found him sitting on a stool, staring at one spot, and emitting short barks at regular intervals. He did not recognize Gorchinsky and growled at him.

The behaviour of Cora, the baboon, was still more curious. After a treatment, she had been sitting in the generator chamber with Komlin, "chatting" quietly with him, when suddenly she jumped violently as if she had received an electric shock. Staring fixedly at some invisible object in the corner of the room, she growled, whimpered and backed away in fright. Komlin tried his best to soothe her, but she would not be comforted. She sat huddled in fear against the wall for a whole hour, her eyes glued to the corner. Now and again she emitted a sharp cry—the danger signal. After a while the attack passed, but Komlin noticed to his surprise that Cora never entered the chamber after that without glancing fearfully at that particular corner.

One day Gorchinsky ran into Komlin's office in great excitement. "Come to the monkey house at once!" he cried. In one of the cages sat a young ape chewing on a banana. There was nothing unusual about the ape or the banana, but both the watchman and Gorchinsky declared they had just witnessed something extremely odd. A few moments before, the ape had been intently watching a slip of paper that had been moving slowly toward it. As the animal reached out its paw to snatch the paper, Gorchinsky had rushed off to fetch Komlin. By the time they returned the paper was gone; the watchman insisted that the monkey had eaten it. At any rate there was no sign of it in the cage. An attempt to reproduce this strange phenomenon had failed.

"Here is what Komlin wrote on that score," said the Director handing the Inspector a piece of graph paper.

"Mass hallucination?" the Inspector read. "Or something quite new? Mass hallucination with the participation of an ape is remarkable in itself. There must be something else here. It is useless to try to find out anything with these animals—monkeys or dogs. I must try it on myself."

This Komlin proceeded to do. Gorchinsky soon found out and lost no time in following suit. They even quarrelled as a result, and in the end Gorchinsky promised not to experiment any more, while Komlin gave his word to try only the simplest, briefest and safest exposures. Gorchinsky did not even know that Komlin had stopped working on neutrino acupuncture.

"Unfortunately," the Director went on, "Komlin's records contain very little information about the truly astounding results of his experiments. His notes become increasingly fragmentary and illegible; one feels he was often at a loss for words to describe his sensations and impressions, and his conclusions are incoherent and diffuse."

The Director had found a few pages torn out of the notebook in which Komlin had described the extraordinary effect on his memory he had noticed after one of his experiments. "It is enough for me to glance at an object once for every detail of it to be stamped with amazing clarity on my memory. I have only to glance at the page of a book to be able to recite it from memory. I have memorized several chapters from *River Backwaters* and the entire table of logarithms from the first to the last figure, and I believe I shall remember them to my dying day. What tremendous possibilities!"

"Memory, as well as many reflexes and habits," he wrote elsewhere in a firm hand, "have a definite material basis that is still unclear to us. This is elementary. The neutrino beam penetrates to this basis and creates new memory, new reflexes, new habits. Or merely causes their appearance indirectly. That is what happened to Genny, Cora and to me (mnemogenesis—the creation of false memory)."

The most interesting and astounding of all Komlin's discoveries were described in the last few pages of notes clipped on to the back of the book.

"Here is the answer to your questions," said the Director, waving these pages at the Inspector.

"This is a sort of synopsis or an outline for a report. Shall I read it?"

"Yes, please."

" 'We cannot even blink by merely willing it. The agency of a muscle is required. The nervous system only plays the part of the carrier of the impulse. This is an infinitesimally small charge, but it is enough to make the muscle contract and shift dozens of kilograms, in other words, perform a colossal amount of work in comparison with the energy of the nervous impulse. The nervous system might be called the detonator in an explosive charge, the muscle the explosive, and the muscular contraction the explosion.

" 'It is common knowledge that an intensification of the thinking process intensifies the electromagnetic fields arising somewhere in the brain cells. Hence biocurrents. The very fact that we can detect them shows that the process of thinking acts on matter—true, not directly, but through the electromagnetic field of the brain. The greater the intensity of the field, the greater the declination of the needle of the device measuring it. Is this not a psychomotor? The electromagnetic field is the brain's muscle.

" 'One develops, for instance, an ability to

calculate at lightning speed. I have done it, but how, I cannot say. I just do it. 1,919×237= =454,803. I got this result in four seconds by the stopwatch. This is all very good, but not the real thing yet. The electromagnetic field is greatly intensified, but what about other fields, if they exist? The muscle is there, but how is one to actuate it?

" 'It works. I have just looked at a tungsten spiral weighing 4.732 grams suspended in vacuum from a nylon strand, and it swung out from its initial position more than fifteen degrees. This is already something. The generator regime. . . .' "

"I spoke to Gorchinsky this evening," said the Director, laying down the papers. "He has seen the vacuum bell jar with the suspended spiral, but it has since disappeared. Evidently Komlin took it apart."

" 'The psychodynamic field—the muscle of the brain—functions,' " he read further. " 'I don't know how it works, and that is not surprising. What does one do to bend one's arm? No one can answer that. To bend my arm I bend it. That is all. But the biceps is a very obedient muscle. Muscles have to be trained. The muscle of the brain must be taught to contract. The question is how?

" 'It is curious, but I cannot lift anything. I can only move things. But not in any specific direction. A match and paper always to the right. Metal toward me. It works best of all with matches. Why?'

" 'The psychodynamic field is effective through glass but not through paper. In order to act on an object I must see it. At the point touched by the field there is a violent disturbance of the air (I presume that is what happens). A match goes out. It seems this can be done at any distance within the bounds of the neutrino chamber.

" 'I am convinced that the potentialities of the brain are inexhaustible. All that is needed is training and activation. In time men will be able to do mental calculations better than any computing machine, and to read and commit to memory a whole library within a few minutes.

" 'It is very exhausting. My head is literally splitting. At times I can work only under constant radiation and toward the end I break out into a sweat. I must take care not to overdo it. Today I am working with matches.' "

The notes ended there.

The Inspector sat with his eyes half closed, thinking. Komlin might well have hit upon an important discovery that would yield rich fruit in time. But in the meantime he was lying in hospital in a critical condition. The Inspector opened his eyes. His glance fell on the fragment of graph paper. " '... You can't do anything with monkeys and dogs. I shall have to try it on myself,' " he read. Could Komlin be right after all?

No, he was not right. He ought not to have taken such a risk, at any rate not on his own. Even when neither machines nor animals can be of any help, a man has no right to play with death. And that is exactly what Komlin had done. And because you, Professor Leman, do not understand this, because you approve of what Komlin has done, you are not fit to head this institute. We cannot let you sacrifice your lives, comrades. In our time we no longer need to take such risks. We can afford to check and double check. In our time your lives are far more precious to us than the most breath-taking discoveries.

Aloud he said: "I think we may consider the investigation closed. The causes of the accident have been ascertained."

"Yes," said the Director, "Komlin collapsed in the act of trying to lift six matches."

* * *

The Director escorted the Inspector to his helicopter. He walked beside the Inspector in silence, lost in thought, and with difficulty matching his pace to the other man's slow, limping gait. As they reached the craft, Alexander Gorchinsky, dishevelled and gloomy, caught up with them. The Inspector shook hands with the Director and climbed painfully into the cabin.

"My old wounds again," he muttered.

"Andrei Andreyevich is much better," Gorchinsky said.

"I know," said the Inspector, settling himself in his seat with a grunt of relief.

The pilot came up at a run and climbed quickly into his place.

"Will you write a report?" Gorchinsky asked.

"Yes," replied the Inspector.

"Hm..." Gorchinsky looked the Inspector in the eye, his whiskers twitching.

"By the way," he said in his high-pitched voice, "are you by any chance the Rybnikov who dealt with some high-explosive gadgets in Kustanai in 1968 without waiting for the automatic equipment to arrive?"

"Alexander Borisovich!" said the Director sharply.

"... That was when your leg was smashed up, wasn't it...."

"That will do, Gorchinsky!"

The Inspector made no reply. He slammed the cabin door and leaned back in his seat.

Gorchinsky and the Director stood on the square watching the big silvery beetle as it floated almost noiselessly over the seventeen-storey pink-and-white stone building of the institute and disappeared in the purple twilight.

Milton Keynes UK
Ingram Content Group UK Ltd.
UKHW041314131223
434301UK00008B/83